Torn Thread

ANNE ISAACS

![Scholastic logo]

SCHOLASTIC
Signature

an imprint of
Scholastic Inc.
New York · Toronto · London · Auckland · Sydney
Mexico City · New Delhi · Hong Kong

To the members of the Buchbinder and Koplowicz families of Bedzin, Poland, who died in the Holocaust between 1943 and 1945, and to Eva Buchbinder Koplowicz and Morris Koplowicz, who alone survive, this book is lovingly dedicated.

ISBN 0-590-60364-7

24 23 22 21 20 19 18 17 16 15 14 13   4 5/0

Printed in the U.S.A.   40

First Scholastic paperback printing, September 2000
The text type was set in 12 point Adobe Garamond.
Book design by Kristina Albertson

THE TRANSLATION FOR PSALM CXLII, ON PAGE 110 (TOP) IS BASED ON *THE NEW ENGLISH BIBLE*, OXFORD UNIVERSITY PRESS AND CAMBRIDGE UNIVERSITY PRESS, 1970.

THE TRANSLATION FOR PSALM CXXI, ON PAGE 110 (BOTTOM) IS BASED ON SHLOMO CARLBACH'S "ESAH EINI", FROM *ZIMRANI* RECORDING, 1959, AND ALSO ON *TANAKH*, PUBLISHED BY THE JEWISH PUBLICATION SOCIETY, 1985.

P A R T   I

June 1943–February 1944

ONE

NIGHT WAS COMING. Wild geese called as they flew toward the mountains. Eva sat cross-legged by the attic window, playing chess with herself. The last daylight touched her face and left a faded patch on the sloping wall beside her. Her sister Rachel paced restlessly across the tiny room, tugging at her hair with a brush.

"You shouldn't exert yourself," Eva said, looking anxiously at Rachel's pale face. "This is your first day out of bed in a week."

"I'm well enough to go outside," Rachel said, but it was more like a question. The room was so small that it took only three steps to cross it, two more to step around the wooden crate that they used as a table.

"Papa said your lungs are still weak," Eva reminded her, as if that settled the matter. Eva turned back to the chessboard, which she had scratched into the wooden floor a month earlier when the Nazis had forced them to move into the Jewish ghetto. For playing pieces she used bits of wood that she picked up from the street, then shaped into castles, knights, and pawns with Papa's pocketknife.

"It's less than four blocks to Auntie's room," Rachel persisted. "You always say that fresh air is good for my lungs."

"Fresh air *would* be good," Eva answered thoughtfully. She looked out the window as if to reassure herself. The glass was stained and cracked, but through it she could see nearly three blocks of Promyka Street which ran at an angle through the middle of the ghetto. It was a warm evening, and the street and sidewalks were filled with people. The crowd was thickest outside the bakery, where women waited for their daily bread rations. At the end of the street a German soldier patrolled the fence that marked the boundary of the ghetto. No Jews were allowed beyond it without a special pass.

A group of young boys ran through the crowd, shouting and tossing a hat back and forth. For a moment Eva envied them, envied their ability to lose themselves in their game. The little boys probably thought it was an adventure to live in the ghetto, where the entire Jewish population of two cities had been forced into a few square blocks.

Beyond the tumbledown tenements of the ghetto, Eva could see part of the center of town, where she had been free to walk only a few weeks ago. The black swastika on a German flag loomed like a gigantic spider above the roof of the old Jewish school, which the Germans had converted to an army barracks. Years ago, when the rising eagle of the Polish flag still flew above the school, Eva and Rachel had been students there. On days as hot as this, Eva and her friends would have taken the long way home to wade in the cool shallows of the river.

"How can I wash my hair if I don't go to Auntie Rivka's?" Rachel pleaded as she stopped her pacing to kneel beside Eva. "Auntie is the only one we know with a sink in her room."

"Wear something warm," Eva gave in at last. "And don't let cousin David wear you out."

"That little angel wear me out?" Rachel replied in cheerful indignation, and immediately went to get her blue-flowered cotton dress from a small pile of clothes under the eaves. She put on the dress and pinned a yellow felt star to the front, just above her heart. *JUDE*, Jew, was printed across the star in black letters.

"Who's winning?" Rachel bent to look at Eva's chess game.

"No one," Eva replied, a little irritably. "I'm managing to lose both sides at once."

"That's hard to do," Rachel observed with a smile. She knelt to take a closer look.

"As you see," Eva said, "the queen is trapped by this castle." She turned the crudely carved little tower in her fingers, remembering the beautiful old synagogue that had stood in the shadow of King Casimir's castle on a little hill at the edge of town. Four years ago, when the German soldiers had marched into Bedzin, their first act had been to set fire to the synagogue. Eva and Rachel had raced home from school in the middle of the morning, crying for Papa and choking on the smoke that filled the streets and turned the bright day into twilight. They had found Papa standing in front of his candy factory, tears running down his face, and had sobbed in his arms while ashes fell from the dark air onto their hair and navy blue school dresses.

"What if you moved this knight over here," Rachel asked, "to take the castle?"

"That would expose the king," Eva said, and set the castle back on the board.

Rachel studied the game a minute longer. "I'm afraid you'll have to wait for Papa," she said finally. She held out her brush and some hairpins. "Would you do my hair? I can't tell what I look like without a mirror."

"You look very much like my sister." Eva began to twist Rachel's red-gold hair into a bun. "Except that your hair is dirty."

"I wish we could go home, even for an hour," Rachel said softly. "Just to stand in the kitchen would be enough."

"It would *not* be enough," Eva told her, frowning as she fastened Rachel's hair in place. She didn't want to think about their home on Zawale Street, where they had lived from the time they were born until one month ago.

"We're caged in like criminals — or dogs," Rachel said.

"It's bad enough being stuck in an attic with no air at the hottest time of the year," Eva complained. "Then you got sick again, naturally, so I couldn't even go out." As soon as the words left her mouth she regretted them.

"Well, I'm better now," Rachel said quietly, but there was an edge of anger in her voice. "I'll stop at the bakery on the way to Auntie's," she added, and took their ration coupon from a dish on the wooden crate.

"I'm sorry, Rachel." Eva went and leaned her head against her sister's. "I don't know what's gotten into me today."

"Fresh air might do *you* some good, too," Rachel said. But she smiled as she added, "If you stare at that chessboard much longer your brain will turn to jam."

"At least we'd have something to put on our bread," Eva replied.

Rachel laughed and started downstairs, and Eva went to straighten Rachel's quilts, which lay in a heap on the floor where she had slept. Eva shook them out and began to fold them, remembering the German soldiers who had sent them from their home on Zawale Street. One soldier had stood in the living room, pointing a gun at Papa, while the other tore through their drawers and cupboards, paying no more attention to her family than if they were specks of lint on the carpet. They had been given less than five minutes to gather clothes and quilts before they were thrown out onto the street, where thousands of Jews were being herded along by soldiers with snarling dogs.

Suddenly Rachel's sweater fell out from one of the quilts. Eva grabbed it and tore downstairs. "Rachel, wait!" Eva caught up with her sister at the front door and held out the sweater.

"But it's summer," Rachel protested. She struggled to push open the tall, wooden door. The soft evening air spilled into the hallway, which smelled of rotting wood. "There! Doesn't it feel good, Eva?"

"Yes, but your hair will be wet, and after it gets dark —"

"Don't be an old auntie," Rachel teased. "I'm not going to the mountains."

Eva hugged the sweater to her chest and watched her sister walk off. She had made the sweater last winter, using wool from an old dress of Mama's. Mama had died in the influenza epidemic five years ago, but sometimes Eva thought she could smell a trace of her mother's perfume in the soft wool.

A light breeze ruffled Eva's hair as she stood in the doorway. Nearby children were singing, clapping their hands in time to the song. For a moment Eva was tempted to run after Rachel, but she held back. In the past week, while Rachel had been sick, Eva had seldom left her side. As much as Eva loved Auntie Rivka, Uncle Nuchem, and little David, she was anxious for some time by herself.

She let the door close behind her, then made her way through the crowd toward the opposite end of the block, where the Jewish cemetery lay just beyond the ghetto fence. Men and women crowded by the fence, weeping, praying, and whispering their thoughts to loved ones who lay beneath the stones. The cemetery was so close that if she had been able to reach through the metal fence, Eva could have almost touched the nearest gravestones. Mama was buried there, as well as Mama's parents and grandparents, but their stones were hidden behind trees and bushes on the far side of the cemetery. Eva made her way along the fence to an old tree whose leafy branches reached over into the ghetto, as if trying to connect the living to the dead. The heavy limbs swayed back and forth like praying men, fanning her with currents of soft air.

Perhaps Rachel was right, Eva thought as she closed her eyes and breathed in the moist freshness of the grassy cemetery. Perhaps she *was* acting like an old auntie, instead of Rachel's younger sister. Still, she couldn't remember a time when she hadn't had to worry about Rachel's health.

Rachel's frequent colds and coughs were often accompanied by high fevers and shortness of breath. More than once, Papa had had to rush Rachel to the hospital when she had all but stopped breathing. Papa had told Eva, again and again, that Rachel's illnesses bore no connection to the one that had killed Mama. Even so, Eva found it impossible to separate the loss of her mother from her fears for her sister.

Eva wrapped the sweater around her, remembering how Mama had tended the ground around her parents' gravestones. She had let Eva dig the holes to plant tiny shrubs whose red berries would show bright against the snow. But while the shrubs had thrived through the winter, Mama had not. And in the spring, Eva had gone alone to the cemetery to plant new shrubs around her mother's grave.

Who would tend it now? Eva thought, hot tears starting in her eyes as she gripped the metal fence.

Just then truck horns blared shrilly in the street. What were trucks doing in the ghetto? Alarmed, Eva pushed her way through the crowd to look.

Two German army trucks drove slowly up Promyka Street and came to a stop. People backed away; mothers lifted children into their arms. Suddenly, soldiers jumped from the trucks and began to seize people, forcing them onto the trucks at gunpoint. Pandemonium broke out at once as everyone raced toward the nearest building or alley, anywhere out of reach of the soldiers.

Unable to resist the tide of people all around her, Eva was swept up and carried backwards into a building, where she was pressed against a wall, nearly unable to breathe. By forcing her way along the wall she managed to catch glimpses from a window. *Rachel, hurry,* she thought. *Get off the street!* Eva looked frantically for her sister as men, women, and children ran past the window, screaming and trampling one another in their desperation to reach a doorway. The crowd on the street grew thinner as people fled or were snatched by the soldiers.

Then Eva saw her in front of the bakery, both arms wrapped around her thin body. Two soldiers ran toward her. Rachel stared at them without moving, as if she had been turned to stone.

"Rachel! Run!" Eva screamed, although there was nowhere for Rachel to go. *"Run!"*

The soldiers shoved Rachel into the back of a truck, then jumped in and slammed the door behind them.

Within seconds the truck made its way to the end of the block, turned a corner, and was gone.

TWO

FOR THREE WEEKS after the raid Eva stayed close to the attic window, praying that Rachel would walk back down the street.

There had been several raids since that first one, and people seldom left their rooms. But even that offered little protection, for the German soldiers tore through the buildings, snatching people from their beds or rooting them out of secret hiding places.

Papa built a false partition along the bottom of the sloping wall in the attic room, using old boards from a storeroom in the basement that blended perfectly with the attic floor and wall. Two small boards could be removed to let Eva and Papa enter the confined space behind the partition, and Papa had moved the large crate over to hide their place of entry.

During the long days without Rachel, Eva unraveled the yarn from both of her sister's sweaters, then knit them over again in new patterns. A surprise for Rachel when she came back, Eva told herself. She focused intensely on her work, as if piecing the strands of yarn together could bring her sister back again.

With every day it became harder for Eva to convince herself that Rachel would return. The Nazis had assigned Papa to a job as an accountant — without pay, since he was a Jew — working for the manager of the German army's regional construction depot. As Papa walked through Bedzin on his way to work each morning he would stop secretly at the house of a former neighbor or friend, or someone who used to work in Papa's candy factory, to ask for their help in finding Rachel. But no one had been willing to help. Afraid to be seen talking with a Jew, or uninterested, they had shut their doors on him.

Finally Papa had summoned his courage to approach Commander Fuhlhaber, the depot manager. To Papa's relief Commander Fuhlhaber agreed to look into the matter, and Eva's hopes had risen. Surely the Nazi manager would find out where Rachel was; perhaps he would arrange for Rachel's return. After all, hadn't Uri Turkow come back to the ghetto a week after he'd been seized in a raid? The Germans had found Uri unsuitable for hard labor because of a weak back, and had sent him home. Clearly Rachel was unfit for hard work of any kind; maybe the Germans would send Rachel home, too.

But still there was no word about Rachel. Every night when Papa came home, he said only, "We must trust in God for help."

Now another day was fading, taking with it another strand of hope. The chess pieces lay abandoned in a corner of the attic, while the sweater Eva was knitting draped over her lap onto the rough floor. It was getting too dark to work by the light from the window, but Eva continued without slackening her pace. She glanced outside. The street below was empty except for an old woman hurrying through the dusk, bent over as if she were heading into a strong wind.

Why had she let Rachel go out by herself? Eva asked herself for the tenth time that day, the hundredth time that week. If she had gone with Rachel she could have pulled her into a building or down an alley, out of reach of the soldiers.

A few pale stars were beginning to show. The constellation Orion appeared above the rooftops, one starry leg raised as if he were trying to leap clear of the city. Almost ten o'clock, Eva thought, noting the position of the stars. Papa would return from work soon.

Eva rose and began to pace around the room. What if Rachel got sick? Who would take care of her? It was Eva's fault that Rachel hadn't brought her sweater. She would have worn it if Eva had insisted.

The street door creaked open, and heavy footsteps sounded in the entry. Instantly Eva froze, alert to every movement, then relaxed as the sound of Uncle Nuchem's deep, rasping cough came up the stairs ahead of him. Eva's face brightened, and she turned to meet him.

"How's my sweet niece?" Uncle Nuchem greeted her, then grimaced as he bumped his head against the sloping ceiling. "We'll have to ask Hitler for better accommodations," he added, wrapping Eva in a tight embrace. "Here's a hug from Auntie Rivka, one from little David, and one from me."

"I wish I could see them more often." Eva blinked back tears as she poured the last glass of water from a pitcher on the table, then offered it to him.

"Any news?" Uncle Nuchem took a sip of water and scanned her face anxiously.

"Papa said he would talk to Commander Fuhlhaber again today."

Uncle Nuchem nodded silently.

"Why can't I stay with you and Auntie?" Eva burst out.

"Don't think we don't worry, knowing you are here alone while your Papa is at work." Uncle Nuchem sat down near the table and drew her close. "Rivka and I talked about having you move in with us, but we think you're safer here, with the hiding place your Papa made."

"You have a hiding place, too."

"And fourteen people to share it, two of them babies. Babies can be a problem if you're trying to —" Uncle Nuchem broke off suddenly, seized by a fit of coughing which went on for several minutes, leaving him breathless and doubled over in pain. Eva stared helplessly at the spots of blood on the handkerchief he'd used to cover his mouth. Uncle Nuchem's illness had gotten much worse, she realized in terror.

Finally, Uncle Nuchem wiped his forehead, finished the glass of water, and leaned his back against the wall, breathing heavily. His face was white.

"Let me get more water from the pump," Eva offered. She took the pitcher and started for the door.

"No, don't go outside!" said Uncle Nuchem, reaching out to stop her. "There's talk about a raid tonight.

"When your Papa comes back," he went on in a hoarse voice, "tell him the Germans made another 'Selection' today. Two hundred people were taken; the soldiers said they'd be resettled on farms in the East." The look on his face told Eva that Uncle Nuchem didn't believe the Germans.

"Rivka will worry if I'm gone any longer," he said apologetically. He handed Eva the glass and stood with an effort.

"Wait — I made something for David," Eva said, trying to smile. She gave Uncle Nuchem a paper propeller fastened to the end of a stick. It whirled with a soft humming sound when she blew on it.

"Thank you, Eva. David will love this," Uncle Nuchem said. He kissed her on both cheeks. "You'll be careful?"

Eva nodded, fighting tears. Uncle Nuchem said this every time he visited her, although they both knew that no amount of carefulness could guarantee their safety.

Eva returned to her place by the window and thought about what Uncle Nuchem had just told her. She picked up her knitting and began to work at a furious pace, without taking her eyes off the street. What if Papa didn't return that evening? What if he had been taken in the Selection?

Over and over Eva told herself that it wouldn't happen. After all, Papa reported directly to Commander Fuhlhaber. *Papa is an essential worker,* she said to herself; *they can't manage without him.* But she knew that to the Germans no Jew was essential.

It was she who couldn't manage without Papa.

Then she saw him. He was walking quickly, his head bent down so that his face was hidden, and only his dark beard showed under the brim of his hat. The street door opened, and Papa's footsteps echoed on the stairs. Eva ran to open the attic door, then threw her arms around him. Papa held her close.

"*Chavele,* my little Eva." Papa stroked her hair as if she were still a little girl, although she was twelve and already as tall as he was.

"Rachel is alive," he said. Eva looked up so quickly, she nearly knocked Papa's hat off, but he added, "She is at a Nazi labor camp in a town called Parschnitz, in Czechoslovakia."

Eva began to weep. Papa led her to the table, where he sat down beside her.

"I believe that Rachel is safe at this camp in Parschnitz," he went on, his voice taut with anxiety and fatigue. "Herr Fuhlhaber told me that the prisoners there work in a factory, making cloth for German army blankets and uniforms. As long as Germany wages war," he added, "they will need clothes and blankets for their soldiers."

That could be a long time, Eva thought fearfully, for she knew that Germany's dictator, Hitler, had sent his armies into almost every country in Europe. Papa had told her over a year ago that the United States had joined the Soviet Union and Britain in their war against Germany; and still there seemed to be no end in sight to the fighting.

"*Chavele*, listen to me," Papa said gently. "It is not safe for you here." Eva clung to Papa as if she could disappear into the folds of his coat. "Do you remember Gregor Toponitzky, who used to work in our factory? He told me about a Nazi camp a half-hour train ride from here, near Auschwitz. Gregor's brother works on the rail lines and saw it for himself. The Nazis take Jews there by train — hundreds, thousands every day — then kill them. It will not be long until they have killed every Jew in Poland."

"Papa, let's run away!" Eva burst out. "We could hide in the forest."

"Even if we got past the ghetto sentries, there are German troops stationed along all the roads."

"You have a work pass," she said weakly, but she knew what Papa would say. They had talked about it — how many times? — since they had moved to the ghetto, and before, while they were still in their home on Zawale Street. "We could go at night," she whispered.

"And how long would we survive in the woods?" Papa replied. "If we didn't starve or freeze to death, the wolves would tear us to pieces — or the Germans would find us first and save them the trouble.

"I have arranged —" Papa began, then stopped for a minute, struggling to control his voice. Finally, he drew Eva close and said very softly, "I have arranged for you to join Rachel."

"No, Papa! No! Let me stay with you!" She buried her face in the familiar warmth of his beard.

"I have no choice, my little one. It is a chance to save your life."

"I don't want to save my life," she said, sobbing. "I want to stay with you."

"Dear *Chavele*." Papa's hands were warm and strong around hers. "Someday the Nazis will be defeated, and we will all be together again. Until then you and Rachel must take care of each other."

Papa rose and lit a candle on the table. In the soft glow he looked pale and tired, but his voice was calm again. "A girl must be thirteen to work at this camp," he said.

"But I'm twelve. How can I —"

"I told them you are thirteen."

Eva looked up. She couldn't remember Papa ever lying before. Nor could she imagine how her sister could take care of her, even though Rachel was two years older.

"Who will take care of *you?*" Eva asked him. "How will you survive?"

"I have plans, *Chavele*. It will be safer for us both if I do not tell you what they are." He stroked his beard, thinking. "Perhaps one thing." He managed a slight smile. "I plan to be here to bless the seven or eight grandchildren you and Rachel bring me."

"Seven or eight each?"

Papa kissed Eva and dried her cheeks with his handkerchief. He took a boiled potato from his pocket and set it on the table beside a large roll, half of their daily ration. There would be nothing else for dinner.

"Have you eaten, *Chavele?*"

"I was waiting for you."

"Then let us thank God together."

Eva joined him: "*Baruch atah Adonai, Elohenu melech ha'olam; ha'motzi lechem min ha'aretz.* Blessed are You, Ruler of the world, Who bring forth bread from the earth."

Eva knew that Papa must have gone to great effort to get a potato, but she could barely swallow it. All she could think was that she would soon be leaving him, perhaps forever.

"When do I go?" Eva struggled to keep her voice steady.

"Seven in the morning, *Chavele.* You will not be allowed any baggage," Papa added. "You must wear as much as you can."

Eva's clothes lay beside Rachel's in a small pile under the eaves. With Papa's help Eva stuffed, tied, and sewed as many of them as she could into a single many-layered garment. She filled the pockets with writing, knitting, and sewing supplies, and photographs of the family. Papa added the two books they had brought with them into the ghetto: a book of daily prayers, and another of psalms. Eva's hands trembled as she sewed the pockets closed.

Then she joined Papa at the window. Queen Cassiopeia had taken Orion's place above the roof across the street. Eva thought about how Papa, Rachel, and she used to walk at night and how Papa would teach them the constellations. Above the dark street the stars seemed to have drawn back farther from the earth.

"Papa, I don't know how to stay alive," Eva said, her voice torn by pain and fear. "I don't know what to do."

Papa was silent for a minute. Then he said, "Even now, there is sometimes a choice, a chance to act. Each choice may not mean much. It may only grant you another hour. But that is one hour closer to the time when we can be together. Whenever you can, ask yourself which choice might keep Rachel and you alive for one more hour."

How will I know, Papa? Eva thought. *How will I know, without you?*

A siren wailed in the distance. Somewhere in the dark streets dogs began to bark. Eva shivered and drew closer to Papa.

"Do not give up, *Chavele*." Papa wrapped his coat around Eva's shoulders. "Promise me that."

Eva nodded, unable to speak.

"We must trust in God —" Papa began, then stopped and held her close without another word.

T H R E E

THE NEXT DAY dawned with a fierce brilliance. Eva put on her layers of clothes while Papa went to the bakery and brought back their bread ration. They ate half of it together, then Papa wrapped the rest for Eva to eat on the train.

Papa showed his work pass and Eva's ticket to the guard at the ghetto gate, and carried Eva's thick wool coat while they walked through town toward the station. Even without the coat Eva felt sticky with sweat and could barely move under all the layers.

They crossed the marketplace in May Third Square, where Polish women haggled over chickens and unloaded cabbages and potatoes from horse-drawn carts. Papa held Eva's hand tightly. As they passed a woman selling eggs and butter, her little boy threw a half-eaten currant bun on the cobblestones and ran off to join some friends. His mother picked up the bun and began to scold him, but when she saw Eva and Papa she fell silent and busied herself counting eggs into baskets. A toothless woman in a ragged black shawl limped toward them. "Dirty Jews," she muttered, and spat on the ground.

The street outside the station was crowded with Poles in bright summer clothes, hurrying past with canvas satchels and brown paper packages under their arms. Papa helped Eva squeeze into her coat. He put his hands on her head and bowed his own.

"May the Lord bless you and keep you —" he began, but a German soldier appeared and grabbed him roughly by the arm. The soldier talked to Papa in German, then called to another soldier, and together they looked at Papa's papers. Before she knew what was happening, Eva was torn from Papa and half-dragged toward the station.

"Papa!" Eva cried. She tried to look back but she could not see him through the crowd.

Inside the station a fenced area was guarded by soldiers. Men, women, and children were penned into the small enclosure. All of them wore yellow stars. Their wailing filled the station.

At first Eva thought the soldier was going to put her into the enclosure with the others, but he pulled her past. For half a second her eyes met those of a girl behind the metal fence, and Eva recognized her, Dvora Hirszcowitz, one of her classmates in the Jewish school.

In back of the station stood a black train. Eva caught a glimpse of a huge engine belching smoke before she was pushed up the metal steps and into a car.

The car was crowded with young Jewish women and girls. The wooden benches were painted black; *like a hearse,* Eva thought. She squeezed onto a seat near a window, hoping by some miracle to catch a glimpse of Papa.

"You're making it impossible to breathe," complained one of the girls on the bench. "Move somewhere else!"

If only I could, Eva thought without taking her eyes from the window; *if only I could move somewhere safe, where there are no Nazis, and take Rachel and Papa with me!*

A few minutes later the train rumbled and squealed, lurched forward, stopped, and finally began to creep from the station. Pressed to the window, Eva watched the familiar streets and buildings of Bedzin pass slowly by. She watched until Bedzin was only a dot on the horizon.

Then she stripped off her extra layers and gathered them into a bundle at her feet. She turned to look around the car, hoping to see someone she knew, but no one looked familiar. Her skin prickled from the heat, and her tongue felt thick and dry. She turned to the girl beside her. "Excuse me," she began, "is there any water —"

"No!" the girl snapped. "Bring any food?" she added roughly. Eva shook her head, startled.

"Then don't bother me!" The girl dismissed Eva with an angry wave of her hand, but someone on the bench in front turned and spoke in a gentler tone.

"There's no food," she explained. "Some of us — it's been days."

Eva nodded, grateful for the girl's kindness. "Is there any water?" she asked quietly.

"Sometimes, at night." The girl fanned herself with a scrap of newspaper. "Know where you're being sent?"

"To Parschnitz, in Czechoslovakia. My sister's at a camp there."

The girl turned so that she could look directly at Eva. "They let you choose? You're lucky."

"What about you?" Eva asked.

The girl shrugged wearily. "If I don't get some food soon . . . who knows . . . ?" her voice trailed off.

It grew hotter as the sun beat down on the train and poured through the windows, which were locked and barred like windows in a prison. The latrine consisted of two pails; they were already full, and women had begun to relieve themselves in corners. As the heat increased, so did the smell.

The train stopped frequently, and more women were herded

on. Sometimes a German soldier would enter the car and read names from a list, and women would get off with him.

They traveled through the night. At one of the stops a soldier brought a pail of water. As soon as he left, dozens of women rushed at the pail; precious water spilled on the floor as they fought each other for a drink.

In the middle of the night, when the others on her bench were asleep, Eva reached into the pocket where she had put her bread. It wasn't there. She searched through all her clothes. She groped under the bench and along the floor. Finally she gave up and sank back on the bench.

All night she listened to women moaning, weeping, praying, and muttering in Polish or Yiddish.

A woman whose face was hidden by a black shawl repeated endlessly, "Pluck her feathers, put her in the pot!" Then she would burst out laughing, as if the words held an immense, secret joke.

Near the front of the car sat a girl with a terrible cough that shook her whole body. Every time she coughed, a girl next to her would bark at her to be quiet.

Eva leaned against the windows and closed her eyes, but she couldn't sleep. Her thoughts drifted back to Bedzin, to the time before the Germans came. She was in Papa's candy factory, decorating chocolate candies; her schoolbooks lay open beside her on the marble counter while she shaped tiny flowers out of frosting. Beside her Rachel wrapped the candies in gold foil and put them into boxes. Papa was nearby at his desk, writing in a ledger. Deliverymen came and went. Shlomo and Yozek, her teenaged cousins, sliced fudge and poured syrup into molds for cough lozenges, clowning and teasing each other the whole time.

She thought back to the bustle on Malachowskiego Street on Friday just before sundown, when men hurried back from the communal steam baths with their hair slicked down and bundles of clothes in their arms, while the smells of chicken soup, raisin-noodle pudding, and potato dumplings wafted from a thousand steam-glazed windows.

Once again she was running on the paving stones, racing her best friend, Tovia, home from school. Mrs. Mandelbaum leaned out from her third-story window to call, "Slow down, girls! Do you want to be good housewives or soccer players?" And Tovia called back, "Are there any other choices, Mrs. Mandelbaum?"

Farther back still, Eva saw her mother listening to opera on the radio, knitting as she sang along in her sweet, wavering soprano.

But there were other memories Eva couldn't block out, no matter how she tried — like the time shortly after the German invasion when Papa had tried to get them all out of Poland. He had traded Mama's jewelry and nearly all of his money for false identity papers and three train tickets to Italy. Papa, Rachel, and Eva went to the station without suitcases and without wearing their yellow stars, just as they had been instructed. But when they showed their papers to the German stationmaster, he roared with laughter and ripped the tickets into shreds.

Later came the night when members of the SS, the dreaded private army of the Nazis, had dragged thousands of Jews from their homes and penned them overnight in the soccer stadium. A freezing rain fell while SS officers walked through the crowds, selecting people for deportation — "to the East," was all they said. When Rachel collapsed, feverish and coughing, Eva lay on top of her to keep her warm, and covered them both with her coat.

Now, in the hot, crowded train car, Eva prayed silently that God would keep Rachel well. She leaned her aching head against the glass, trying not to think what might await her at the labor camp. As the train entered a forest, dark, twisted shapes sped past her window like demonic messengers. The train slowed as it wound around the side of a hill and began to climb.

Hour by hour, town by town for two days, as the train crawled through the mountains from Poland to Czechoslovakia, she begged God to take care of Papa.

F O U R

HALFWAY THROUGH THE third day the train stopped in a thick stand of fir trees. A guard got on and read a list of names; Eva's was among them. With every limb stiff and aching, Eva stumbled down a steep embankment to join the girls who had gotten off before her. She looked around for a station building or signs of a nearby town, but all she saw was a dirt path leading into the trees. The acrid smells of coal smoke and burnt oil stung her nostrils.

Surely now they would get something to eat and drink, Eva thought desperately as guards prodded the girls with rifles and shouted at them to line up. Surely the guards could see how tired and weak they were.

"Marsch!" the guards shouted, and the girls began to march down the path. "*Schneller!* Faster!"

Stiff and sore from days of sitting on the crowded benches, they stumbled awkwardly as they hurried on the uneven path.

"Dirty swine!" a guard shouted when one of the girls tripped and fell.

After a short distance the path widened to a dirt road with tracks worn by wagons. The girls followed the road out of the trees and down a hill toward a wide valley filled with fields of corn, and meadows where sheep grazed. A range of high mountains rose in the distance.

They passed a farmhouse and barn, and a stone silo whose thatched roof was shaped like the cap of an acorn. Road signs pointing to ski resorts in the Giant Mountains reminded Eva of the lodge, in these same mountains, where Papa had taken them four years earlier to bathe in the healthful mineral spas. It had been their last vacation, for the German army had marched into

Bedzin only days after their return. Her hunger sharpened as she remembered the tiny cakes with pink frosting she and Rachel had eaten at the lodge.

The girls' feet raised clouds of dust that made Eva choke. There had been fountains of mineral water at the mountain lodge, she remembered. Rachel and Eva had held their noses, breaking into giggles whenever Papa had offered them a glass; now she'd have traded everything she owned for one sip of the foul-smelling water.

The sun beat down, unbroken by any shade. More than once Eva considered throwing aside her bundle as other prisoners had done, but she clung to it mechanically. She carried it until her arms ached, then draped the heavy clothes over her shoulders.

Her shoes were too small and pinched her toes painfully. She hadn't had a new pair in two years, and her feet had grown. Now it felt as if she were walking on coals. Eva plodded on, aware of little more than hunger, thirst, and the burning in her feet. Her legs no longer seemed to be part of her body, but moved along as if by their own will.

She began to listen to her fears. What if Rachel wasn't in the camp at Parschnitz? A tiny voice whispered that there was no Parschnitz, that the guards would make them walk until they dropped and were buried in their own dust.

What if Rachel was dead?

At last a cluster of rooftops appeared beyond the cornfields, with tall smokestacks towering above them like raised fists.

Then the dirt road gave way to cobblestones, and shops and houses began to appear on either side of the road.

The prisoners arrived at a group of long, three-story brick buildings surrounded by a high brick wall with barbed wire at the top. The guards led them through the gate into an open, unpaved yard with a row of latrines in the middle. While the prisoners lined up before a table, a female officer in a black suit observed them with a face of stone. The white skulls on her uniform marked her as an officer of the SS.

"Your name?" a guard at the table asked the first girl.

"L-Leni Barber," she stammered.

The guard wrote in a ledger, then held out a round metal tag on a string. "Read it — out loud!" she ordered.

"39227," read the girl.

"From now on *that* is your name," said the guard. "Put it around your neck! Memorize it!" She pointed to one of the three-story buildings. "Barracks 2."

The prisoner hesitated for a second.

"Go!" another guard said, and pushed the girl toward the building.

Each prisoner was given a numbered tag and assigned to a barracks. "Memorize your number!" the guard at the table said over and over. "Wear your tag at all times!"

When it was her turn, Eva was so frightened that she could barely speak, but she managed to stammer Rachel's name and ask if she might be assigned to her sister's barracks. The guard glanced at her sharply, then searched through a list and pointed at a building.

"Thank you," Eva whispered, relief mixing with fear. She turned and hurried across the hard-packed ground.

When Eva entered the barracks she found herself in a hallway lined with large sinks. She dropped her bundle and took a long drink, then turned to a woman who was washing clothes in a sink nearby.

"Excuse me," she said, "I'm looking for my sister Rachel —"

"There are seven hundred women in here," the woman interrupted her. "At least fifty Rachels. You expect me to know which one is your sister?"

Leaving the hall through a double set of doors, Eva entered an enormous room where three-level wooden bunks were crowded together in two rows running the length of the room. The center aisle was filled with tables, leaving almost no space to walk. Girls and young women gathered anywhere they could, talking to each other in Polish, Yiddish, Czech, and German. Wet clothing was hung or spread to dry in every free corner. Eva made her way through the room, asking everyone she passed if they knew her sister.

"Maybe she's in the next barracks," one girl suggested.

"Or in the next world," another girl added with a sharp laugh, but others quickly hushed her.

"Pay no attention to her," said the first girl. "Have you looked on the second or third floors?"

Eva went slowly through each floor, holding her bundle to

her chest as she squeezed through the tight maze of tables and bunks. Now and then she saw someone across the room with red-blond hair, or heard a voice that sounded like Rachel's, but as Eva got closer it always turned out to be a stranger. No one she asked had heard of her sister.

On the third floor Eva dropped her bundle and collapsed on a bench to rest. She wiped tears and sweat from her face with the back of her hand. Perhaps the guard had sent her to the wrong barracks. Perhaps she had searched too hastily.

Then Eva noticed a thin, blond girl passing a window, her hair lighting up to a coppery color as the sun fell on it. She wore a white dress with blue flowers.

"Rachel?" Eva called hoarsely, rising to her feet. Rachel turned and cried out, then the two sisters hurried into each other's arms.

"Oh, Eva, I thought I'd never see you again," Rachel said. They held on to each other tightly and wept together. For a few minutes neither of them could speak.

"I dreamed that you came," Rachel whispered at last. "Did you get my letter? Where's Papa — is he all right?"

"He's well," Eva said. "He sends his love." She was barely able to speak, for the misery and pain that swelled in her throat.

Rachel took Eva to her bunk and brought her a metal cup filled with water. Eva drank it greedily, then pulled her shoes off her blistered feet and lay down on the straw-filled mattress.

"You look tired," Eva said.

"I'm fine, really. But you don't look well."

"I haven't had anything to eat for three days."

"My God," Rachel said helplessly. "And I have nothing to give you." She explained that rations were not given out on Sundays; Eva would have to wait until the next morning to eat.

Rachel stroked Eva's cheek soothingly. "How are Uncle Nuchem, Auntie, little David?"

"They're well, all of them," Eva said, registering the coolness of her sister's hand and taking in Rachel's pale cheeks and bloodshot eyes with a practiced glance. "You've been sick."

"Only a little, and only at night," Rachel said.

"Have you been coughing?"

"Nothing to mention."

Eva relaxed a little at this. "I brought your clothes," she told Rachel. "Your sweater, your coat, everything I could carry."

Rachel nodded, her eyes filling with tears. She lay down beside Eva on the narrow bunk and rested her head on Eva's shoulder. Eva held her close.

"Tell me, Rachel," Eva whispered, "how bad is it here?" But Rachel only wept and squeezed her hand.

"Inspection!" someone shouted suddenly from the doorway. The message traveled quickly from bunk to bunk.

"Eva! Get up!" Rachel sprang up and handed Eva her shoes, explaining in a frightened voice that Frau Hawlik — the *Lagerführerin,* camp commander — was coming to inspect the barracks.

All around them girls raced to smooth mattresses and blankets, comb their hair, or put wet clothing into one of the narrow wooden lockers that lined the outer walls of the room.

Just then a tall girl with broad shoulders and thick glasses came and spoke quietly to Rachel, who handed over Eva's bundle. The girl grabbed it and hurried off, but Eva was too confused and frightened to ask questions.

Eva washed her face at one of the hall sinks, hastily dampened her hair and smoothed the waves over her forehead. Then she and Rachel joined the girls who were lining up in the center of the room where tables had been pushed to one side to create an aisle.

"Pinch your cheeks to give them color," Rachel whispered anxiously, pinching her own as she spoke. "You have to look strong, show Frau Hawlik you're able to work." Eva quickly followed her example.

Soon a tall, plump woman about thirty years old strode into the room, barking at girls as she went past: "Straighten up, monkey! Comb your hair again — do you think this is a brothel?" She was dressed in a fresh-looking linen dress and, in spite of her plumpness, had a protruding chin and sharp, pointed features. She seemed older than almost anyone else, and walked among the girls as if she were their queen.

"That's Bella Slonimski," Rachel whispered when the plump woman was out of hearing. "She's the *Blockälteste,* the barracks supervisor." Bella was Jewish and lived in the barracks, Rachel added, but she worked for the Nazis, and was meaner than some of the guards. She had a room of her own on the first floor, where she even had a flush toilet.

After a few minutes, several female guards stamped into the room and, along with Bella, began to search among the bunks and lockers, overturning mattresses and blankets, throwing clothes around as they went. Soon the immaculate room looked as if it had been swept through by a hurricane.

"Clean it up! *Schnell!* Fast!" shouted the guards when they were done, and the girls raced to restore order. In less than two minutes the prisoners were back in line in the center of the room.

Loud steps rang in the hall outside. Fear rippled through the line of waiting girls.

"*Achtung!* Attention!" shouted a guard, and Bella and the guards scurried to the entrance of the room just in time to salute Frau Hawlik, the *Lagerführerin,* when she marched in. Frau Hawlik wore an SS officer's uniform, and her pale, almost colorless hair was pulled back tightly under her skull-emblazoned cap. Her eyes were the blue-gray of shadows on snow. She was followed closely by the assistant commander, the stone-faced SS officer Eva had seen in the yard earlier.

The room was silent except for the tapping of Frau Hawlik's polished leather boots on the concrete floor. Bella smiled nervously, bowing her head in deference as she stepped forward to give Frau Hawlik a piece of paper. Then she spoke to the *Lagerführerin* in a low voice, pointing at two short girls with curly red hair. Frau Hawlik took the paper and turned toward the girls, whose faces were so alike that Eva guessed they must be twins. They couldn't be much older than eleven, Eva thought; perhaps their father, too, had lied about their ages. As Frau Hawlik fixed her icy gaze on them, one of the girls began to tremble visibly.

"Let everyone see it!" Frau Hawlik shouted, passing the paper to the assistant commander as she marched toward the red-haired twins.

The stone-faced assistant walked slowly down the line of prisoners, holding up a photograph of a middle-aged woman.

Suddenly Frau Hawlik shouted, "Jews are not to take gifts from citizens of the Reich!" The twin who had been trembling began to cry. The other twin stood perfectly still and betrayed no emotion. With elaborate slowness, Frau Hawlik took a paper bag from her pocket, selected a piece of candy, and ate it, all the while staring at the twins as if she were watching insects in a cage.

"Read it!" Frau Hawlik told the assistant commander.

"'With love from your second mother!'" read the assistant. Then she tore the photograph into pieces and dropped them on the floor.

"What else have you taken from this 'second mother'?" Frau Hawlik shouted. "Potatoes? Socks? *What else?*" The twins said nothing; one of them choked on her tears.

Frau Hawlik went back to the beginning of the line and resumed her inspection of the prisoners. Her leather boots creaked as she walked, and the tapping came closer. Eva kept her eyes lowered.

And then Eva inhaled an aroma she hadn't smelled in years: butterscotch. Instantly she thought of Papa, stirring a copper pot with a long-handled wooden spoon. Without thinking, Eva raised her head and found herself looking straight into the eyes of the *Lagerführerin.*

"A new one," said Frau Hawlik.

Eva's heart pounded.

"Where are you from?" Frau Hawlik held her bag of candy practically underneath Eva's nose.

"Bedzin, Poland," Eva whispered.

"Bedzin," Frau Hawlik repeated. She put a piece of candy in her mouth and began to chew.

"Do you have family in Bedzin — alive?" Frau Hawlik smiled.

Eva forced herself to nod.

"Did you bring any blankets or linens?"

"No, Frau Hawlik."

"Louder!"

"No, Frau Hawlik."

"Write to your family. Tell them to send you blankets and coats. Write soon," she added, and went on to the next prisoner.

FIVE

"WELCOME TO THE Parschnitz palace," said the tall, broad-shouldered girl who had taken Eva's bundle before the inspection. She tossed it back on the bunk and sat down beside Eva.

"This is Kayla Rubenstein," Rachel said, introducing Eva to the tall girl. "She's been here since the camp opened. She knows everything about — everything."

"Except how to get out of here," Kayla replied. "I had to keep your clothes out of Bella's sight," she told Eva, "in case you had anything she might be interested in." Bella took whatever she wanted from the other girls, Kayla explained; no one dared to stop her.

"Hide the photographs someplace when everyone's asleep," Kayla advised Eva in a whisper. "I'm sorry I can't offer you candy," she added in a louder voice, giving Eva a small piece of bread. "I *am* expecting a shipment any day, and I'll be glad to share it when it arrives." She threw back her head and laughed at her own joke.

Eva tried to thank her, but Kayla smiled and waved off her

thanks. "I kept a needle and some thread from your supply," she said, peering at Eva over the top of her thick glasses. "They'll be more useful than gratitude."

"Why would Frau Hawlik tell me to send home for blankets and coats?" Eva asked as she chewed on the bread Kayla had given her.

"A blanket is worth a lot on the black market," Kayla said. "She's probably looking for things to trade for candy. I wouldn't worry about it," she added. "Frau Hawlik always asks new prisoners for things like that." Eva was struck by Kayla's air of casual authority.

"I don't think a letter would reach Papa, anyway," Eva went on. "No one got mail in the ghetto."

"True, but Frau Hawlik reads every letter that enters or leaves the camp, so you'd better send it," Kayla advised. "You can leave it at the office of Fräulein Kirschlag, the assistant commander, in the morning."

Eva took off her shoes and socks again to relieve her feet.

"You're going to have trouble walking to the factory on those blisters," Kayla observed.

"Don't we work here, at the camp?" Eva asked, looking up anxiously.

"The factory's in Trutnov, five kilometers away," Rachel told her. "A train takes us halfway; then we walk the other half."

"The Nazis didn't want us living too near the factory," Kayla explained. "In Trutnov we'd be surrounded by Czechs, who hate them, and might help us escape." On the other hand, she told

Eva, most people in Parschnitz were German, and would kill any Jew who tried to escape.

Eva only half-listened to what Kayla was telling her. She was thinking about her feet, and about the long walk to Trutnov.

"Isn't there some way I could take a day off to let my feet heal?" she asked.

"Where do you think you are, a resort?" Kayla said with a laugh. "It's true that we have an infirmary, and both doctors are Jewish women; but believe me, you don't want to go there.

"Inspections," Kayla added in a low voice. "Worse than in the barracks." Special SS inspectors made unscheduled visits to the camp, she explained; not even Frau Hawlik had any idea when they were coming. The inspectors made everyone in the infirmary do push-ups, and any girl who couldn't — Kayla left the sentence unfinished.

"A shoemaker comes here every Sunday morning," Rachel added quickly, anxious to change the subject. "Maybe next Sunday he can fix your shoes so they don't hurt so much."

"Come and meet Rachel's sister, just arrived from Bedzin," Kayla called to two girls who were passing by. "This is Dora and Rosie Wiseman, from Lodz," Kayla introduced them, and they squeezed onto the bunk beside her.

Dora and Rosie were cousins, Eva soon learned. They were strikingly beautiful. Everything about them, from their prominent noses to their high foreheads and molded cheekbones, looked as if it had been planned by a sculptor. They were shorter than Eva, with dark complexions and green eyes fringed with long lashes, and might have been taken for twins if it weren't for their obvious difference in age. Dora's graying hair, stooped back, and the deep lines around her eyes made her appear much older than her eighteen years, and Rosie seemed younger than fourteen.

Rosie smiled readily and spoke in a sweet, melodious voice that contrasted with the sadness in her eyes. "You don't look a thing like your sister," she told Eva, "although you do have the same brown eyes," she decided, leaning closer to look.

"They're Papa's eyes," Eva told her, "and I got his dark hair, while Rachel's hair is like Mama's."

"Dora's hair is our calendar," said Rosie sadly. "A gray hair for every day we've been apart from our families." She kissed her cousin's head. "I hope there won't be many more," she added quietly.

Dora nodded with her eyes lowered.

"We each have a younger brother," Rosie explained. "My brother, Jakob, was seven when we left, while her brother, Moshe, was ten."

"A year ago, in March, everyone in the ghetto was called into an open square," Rosie went on. "Dora and I were ordered to one side with the older children and young adults; our parents and brothers went to the other. I begged a guard to give Jakob his coat, which I had been holding for him. But the guard laughed and said that where my brother was going, he wouldn't need a coat." Rosie began to weep.

"Anything is possible," Rachel said gently, taking Rosie's hand. "When I came here I thought I'd never see my sister again — and now she's here. You have to believe that your brothers are alive."

"She's right, Rosie," Dora said, pleading. She wiped her own tears and tried to comfort her cousin, but Rosie shook her head and cried inconsolably.

"Your Moshe," Rosie said between sobs, "such a kindhearted boy, as smart as a twenty-year-old. Always scheming, figuring out how to get through the ghetto fence so he could trade bits of clothing in the town to bring us bread and cheese. He kept us all alive when they took away our ration cards, after Papa got sick."

"Maybe the rest of the family stayed together," Dora said.

"In some camps there are special barracks for young children," Kayla offered encouragingly, and Rosie stopped crying to listen. "I've heard that sometimes the Nazis put children to work on farms in Germany, where they get fresh air and good food. There's always a chance. If I could get out of Auschwitz, anything can happen."

"You were in Auschwitz?" Eva asked in horror.

"Yes, and Parschnitz is a fine hotel by comparison," Kayla said. She rubbed her forehead as if trying to erase a painful memory. "The first night I was in Auschwitz, someone stole the shoes off my feet while I was asleep."

"Couldn't you find out who did it?" Rachel asked.

"It wasn't so easy. There were hundreds of women in each

barracks, and the floor was nothing but mud. Outside, more mud, everyone sinking up to her ankles and knees. All the shoes looked the same, covered with mud.

"To get another pair I'd have to steal some myself, or wait until someone died in her sleep." She let her breath out with a shudder. "At Auschwitz you didn't have to wait long. Flu, typhus, you name it: half the women who shared my sleeping platform died the week I came."

"Thank God you got out alive!" said Rachel.

"I don't think God had much to do with it," Kayla replied, and she told them how she had jumped forward the first time the guards had asked for volunteers to work at another camp.

Rachel, Eva, and their new friends stayed together for the rest of the day and were still talking when a siren wailed for the prisoners to go to bed. Then Rachel put on a nightgown Eva had brought, and they lay down on neighboring bunks. The bunks were so close that when Eva rolled over on the straw-filled mattress, her knees touched the edge of Rachel's bunk. Sharp pieces of straw poked Eva through the mattress no matter how she moved, and the coarse wool blanket scratched her skin.

"I'm frightened for Papa," Rachel whispered as she pulled the blanket to her chin. In the dim light that came through the windows, Rachel looked more frail than ever.

"Papa is still young and strong," Eva said, hoping that she sounded more confident than she felt. "And he's smart; didn't he manage to send me here to be with you?"

Rachel squeezed Eva's hands. "Still, I can't bear to think of him all alone."

"He'll be safer this way," Eva replied, struggling to keep her voice steady. "It will be easier for him to hide." Or escape, she added to herself.

"I'm afraid you'll disappear," Rachel said a minute later. "Promise me you'll still be here in the morning."

"I'll be here." Eva leaned over and kissed Rachel's cheek. It seemed to her that it was Rachel who might disappear; she was fading already.

Eva waited until everyone nearby was asleep, then quietly put her photographs in one of her long, woolen stockings and tied it around her waist. The whole family would be there, day and night, close to her heart.

After that Eva lay awake for a long time, thinking back to their last holiday in the mountains. Papa, Rachel, and she had gone for a walk and had climbed a steep trail for several hours. At one point Papa and Rachel stopped to catch their breath while Eva went on ahead. As she rounded a bend in the trail Eva found herself looking up at a high cliff. To her left a rock-slide had covered the trail with a jumble of boulders as large as peasants' huts. To her right lay a thicket of brambles. There did not seem to be a way to get around it, but scaling such a cliff was impossible. Rachel and Papa caught up with Eva, and they all looked awhile in silence. Finally Papa said, "The solution is simple. Either we will find a path around, or God will teach us how to fly."

Eva feared that she couldn't trust her fate, or her sister's, to God alone. It seemed to her that God had not heard the prayers of the Jews for a long time. Besides, she didn't think that God could give them wings.

But what if there was no path around? How would she and Rachel survive here? A cold feeling of dread settled in Eva's stomach; she curled into a ball and pulled the blanket tighter.

Just then the barracks door crashed open. Lights went on with a blinding glare. Guards stormed into the room and took away the red-haired twins.

"Rachel!" Eva whispered after they had gone and the lights had been switched off again. "What will happen to them?"

Before Rachel could answer, the woman in the bunk above her leaned over and whispered one word: "Auschwitz."

S I X

"EVA! WAKE UP!"

A saucer-shaped moon showed through the dark window near the foot of Eva's bunk. Rachel was beside her, fully dressed. Lights glared down, and women moved silently about the room.

"It's still night," Eva protested drowsily as she blinked at her sister.

"It's five-fifteen," Rachel replied. "The food line is getting long." Instantly Eva threw off her blanket and stepped onto the cold floor. Overnight her blisters had broken, exposing raw, pink skin beneath. Eva gritted her teeth as she pulled on her shoes. "What about them?" she asked, noticing that many women were still asleep.

"They work on the night shift. Hurry," Rachel added, handing Eva her dress. "We have to leave the camp at six."

Eva raced to put on her clothes and comb her hair, urged on by the thought of food. As they left the barracks Rachel handed Eva a metal cup, spoon, and bowl. Eva didn't ask where she'd gotten them, afraid that they had once belonged to one of the red-haired twins.

An icy wind whipped at them the moment they stepped outside, as if the season had changed from summer to winter overnight. Rachel shivered under the coat Eva had brought, and Eva's thick sweater seemed to let in the wind through a hundred holes. Guards patrolled the yard, which was lit by yellow lamps on tall poles. Long lines of prisoners waited to use the foul-smelling latrines, while another, seemingly endless line wound through the camp toward the kitchen. Silent, huddled in the shadows under shawls and blankets, the prisoners looked more like ghosts than people.

Rachel pointed out the buildings as she and Eva walked to the back of the line: the large, brick barracks were for prisoners; the smaller ones for guards. In addition, there were camp kitchens, storage sheds, a garage, and an ammunition depot. The depot was rumored to hold enough explosives to destroy the entire town of Parschnitz.

At one end of the camp there was a large open square — the *Appellplatz,* assembly place — where the prisoners were counted every morning before they left camp, and every evening when they came back. A small wooden building at one end of the square housed the prisoners' infirmary.

In the center of the camp stood the white gabled house of the *Lagerführerin,* which Frau Hawlik shared with Fraulein Kirschlag, the assistant commander. The house was surrounded by rows of flowers and a painted wooden fence, in sharp contrast to the bare mud yard and looming brick buildings on all sides. As Eva and Rachel passed the house, a sturdy, red-cheeked girl in a black housemaid's dress came out the front door.

Eva looked enviously at the maid's new leather boots, and was surprised when Rachel told her that the girl was Jewish. The maid seemed so much healthier and better fed than any of the rest of them.

If only I could find a job like the maid's, Eva thought, *Rachel and I would have plenty to eat, maybe even hot showers every day.* Eva watched the maid cross the yard, imagining how it would be, until someone shoved her from behind and growled at her to move forward.

Eva and Rachel carried their rations into the barracks and ate them at a table near their bunks. The coffee had been made from ground chicory roots, and was so bitter that Eva could barely make herself swallow it. The soup was a watery, flavorless broth with pieces of carrots, cabbage, and potatoes. It was already cold by the time they got it, and an oily film coated the surface. The loaf of bread and wedge of cheese Eva had been given looked huge to her, until Rachel explained that they were only given out every three days and had to be carefully rationed. Reluctantly Eva ate a thin piece of bread with a thinner slice of cheese, and wrapped another portion to take with her to the factory, then stored the rest in the locker she shared with Rachel.

Except for the crumbs of bread Kayla had given her the night before, this was the first food Eva had eaten in three days. The scanty meal only seemed to sharpen her hunger.

Sitting on her bunk, Eva wrote a brief letter to Papa, then followed Rachel out to the yard. They stopped at Fräulein Kirschlag's office to deposit the letter before joining their friends in the *Appellplatz,* where the girls lined up to be counted. Eva couldn't help wishing that Papa would see her letter, and that — impossible as she knew it was — she might get a letter from him.

She breathed on her hands to warm them while guards walked up and down the long rows of prisoners, counting them over and over. The red-haired twins seemed to be forgotten, Eva noticed with discomfort. She had not heard anyone mention them that morning, as if there were an unspoken agreement among the prisoners.

"*Mach schnell!* Make it quick!" the guards shouted as they herded the girls toward a small station behind the camp, and onto a train which was waiting.

Eva and Rachel squeezed onto a bench beside Kayla, Dora, and Rosie. Boards were nailed across the outside of all the windows, with narrow spaces between them. Eva pressed her face against the glass and looked out through the spaces. As the train began to move, the houses, stores, and factories of Parschnitz passed slowly by, gray and silent. It was nearly sunrise. Papa would be waking in the attic.

Eva closed her eyes, remembering the tiny dark room with its uneven floor and steeply pitched ceiling, the wooden crates they had used as furniture. She had cried for days when they'd first moved there. Now she gladly would have agreed to live in the ghetto for the rest of her life, if only she and Rachel could be back with Papa.

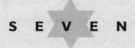

S E V E N

THE VALLEY WAS thick with fog when the train pulled into the Trutnov station. Fog washed over the buildings of the town and clung to the branches of trees, softening edges like an old photograph. The train's smokestack pushed up great white mounds of smoke that hovered in the cold air for a moment before melting into the general grayness.

"*Schnell!* Hurry!" shouted the guards as the prisoners got off, and they pushed the girls with the butts of their rifles. "Five to a row! Faster!"

Rachel and Eva linked arms with Dora, Kayla, and Rosie so they wouldn't be separated. Guards stationed themselves along the line at regular intervals and shouted at the prisoners to march. They filed past the train depot and across a bridge. A river rushed below.

From the bridge Eva could dimly make out part of the main square of Trutnov, its red roofs and stone towers indistinct in the fog. The town appeared to end abruptly a hundred meters from the river. Other than the station there were no buildings of any size near its banks.

The prisoners turned onto a stone-paved walkway lined by giant chestnut trees. The walkway followed close beside the swollen river, which churned noisily over a series of rapids. Pools of glassy water swirled darkly just before they dropped into foaming cascades. Red clay cliffs rose sharply on the opposite bank, and beyond them, dark rows of forested hills. The air smelled of blossoms and damp earth.

"Breathe deeply, Rachel," Eva said. "This is food for the lungs!"

"Perhaps you won't mind giving us your bread," said Kayla, "since you have enough air for a feast?"

A small mill stood on the riverbank ahead of them, its large wooden wheel turning slowly in the water. The square stone building was half-buried by overgrown bushes. As the first prisoners passed the mill, an old woman stepped suddenly from behind a bush, threw a small parcel toward them, then disappeared.

The parcel landed on the walkway. The eyes of every prisoner were on it, but no one moved to pick it up.

A guard ran to get it. "Bread — and roast chicken!" he cried, opening the parcel and holding it above his head. "Who dropped this?"

The only reply was the sound of the river.

"Would you like it?" He thrust the food in front of a girl and forced her to smell it. More guards came, grinning.

"Aren't you hungry?" cried the first guard, pulling another girl from the line. She cringed and shook her head. The guard pushed her away.

"Who wants bread and chicken?" the guard roared.

"Murderer," Rosie whispered, her eyes glittering with rage. "He looks like the one who took —"

"Hush, Rosie," Dora whispered, looking around anxiously. "You mustn't let anyone hear you."

Rosie bit her lip.

They had almost reached the mill. Eva's legs felt as if they had turned to wood. She held Rachel's hand.

"No one's hungry?" The guard's voice rose shrilly. "We're feeding you Jews too well!" The other guards laughed.

"Don't look," whispered Rachel, holding tightly to Eva's hand. Her voice was trembling.

They passed the mill. For a few minutes they heard the

guards taunting prisoners behind them. Finally their voices were lost beneath the sound of the water.

Sharp pains stabbed Eva's feet. How many steps until they reached the factory? Until their workday ended and they returned to Trutnov? The week stretched ahead like an endless series of painful steps, until far-distant Sunday, when the shoemaker would come to the camp and fix her shoes.

"I wonder where we'd be now, Rosie," Dora said dreamily, "if we'd run away to the forest, like we used to talk about. Maybe we'd have found our way to the sea, and a boat for Palestine."

"Or maybe you'd have ended up here, anyhow, like I did," said Kayla. "I hid in the forest for three weeks, not far from a farm. A herd of cows sometimes wandered near my hiding place, so I had milk to live on, as well as berries. I might still be there if the farmer hadn't found me and turned me over to the Nazis."

"What happened to your family?" Eva asked her.

"We had a farm two hours outside of Warsaw — my parents, six brothers and sisters, and two grandparents. After the Germans came we got almost nothing for our crops, and we were forced to sell our few valuable possessions to survive. I was the fastest runner in the family, and the toughest at a bargain, so I was the one who went into Warsaw to trade on the black market. One day when I came home, the house was empty. A Polish neighbor told me that the Nazis had come, along with the Polish police, and had led my family to the woods, where they had shot them into a ditch and buried them. She told me to run, before the police came back and found me. So I ran for five days. On the sixth, I hid in the forest near the cows." Kayla let out a long breath. "You know the rest," she concluded quietly.

The girls walked in silence as the walkway led them away from the river and across an open field, while the sun struggled to break through the drapery of fog. At the far end of the field stood a group of long factory buildings surrounded by a brick wall. HAASE TEXTILES was written in iron letters above the gates. Czech women poured into the gates, coming from the town.

Just then, several rows ahead of Eva, one of the prisoners fainted. Instantly, guards dragged her toward a German army truck parked outside the factory. They threw her in the back like a sack of flour; her body landed with a soft thud.

"Don't slow down," Dora warned Eva in a low voice. They had almost reached the factory gates.

A guard passed, eating bread and chicken.

"The Jews should have fought back when there was still a chance!" Kayla whispered angrily as they stopped inside the gates a minute later.

"When was there a chance?" said Rachel.

"Maybe it's time now," Kayla snapped.

Women hurried past on their way to work.

"Hush! A guard's coming," said Rachel, and immediately Kayla, Dora, and Rosie ran off. Rachel led Eva across the yard to the factory employment office, where she hugged Eva good-bye and hurried after the others.

The office was crowded with women waiting to be assigned jobs. Two German guards sat behind a desk at one end, chatting as if they hadn't noticed anyone else. Women and girls, Czech and Jewish, spread freely throughout the room, despite a sign that restricted Jews to one side, "Reich citizens" to another.

A Czech girl stood next to Eva with a small loaf of bread sticking out of a cloth sack she had slung across her shoulder. Eva's mouth watered as she gazed at the bread.

Just then a tall, heavy man in a crumpled green business suit came in and forced his way through the crowd to Eva. He was out of breath, and his face glistened with beads of sweat.

"Come with me!" he ordered in German, and pushed Eva ahead of him toward the guards.

"This one has been assigned to Flax Spinning," he announced briskly, as if he was used to giving commands.

"Yes, sir, Herr Schmidt!" One of the guards sat up quickly and pulled a thick ledger toward him. "Her name?" he added.

"Eva Buchbinder," Herr Schmidt growled, and wiped his face with a large handkerchief.

A chill ran through Eva. How did he know her name?

"Number?" the guard asked as he wrote in the ledger.

"Tell him!" Herr Schmidt commanded.

"39267," Eva said, her voice shaking.

The official wrote in the book, then saluted Herr Schmidt. *"Heil Hitler!"* he said.

"Heil Hitler," replied Herr Schmidt, saluting in return.

"Quickly!" he barked at Eva, and pulled her outside.

EIGHT

HERR SCHMIDT LED Eva across a courtyard and into a building. He loped awkwardly but he was long-limbed, and Eva had to run to keep up. A steady humming noise filled the long corridor inside the building, as if they had entered a gigantic hornet's nest. Herr Schmidt stopped beside a stairway to check his watch.

"Fourth floor," he told Eva gruffly, wiping his face again, then his entire head with his handkerchief. His scalp was covered with sparse brown and gray stubble, like a scrub brush that had lost most of its bristles.

"Go!" he shouted, waving impatiently at the stairs with his handkerchief.

On the way upstairs Herr Schmidt puffed along beside Eva, leaning heavily on the rail and stopping frequently to gasp for breath. Where was he taking her, Eva worried, and how did he know her name?

The humming noise grew louder with every floor. On the fourth floor the stairs ended abruptly beside a metal door with

FLAX SPINNING painted on it in black letters. Herr Schmidt checked his watch, then pulled out his handkerchief and mopped his face again. His large square face was very red.

"Good, good; just in time," he muttered to himself. The steady droning had grown so loud that Eva could barely hear him. "Your sister Rachel told me you were here," he said then. "I promised her I'd look after you."

Before Eva could get over her surprise, Herr Schmidt opened the door, and the humming exploded into a roar as loud as a dozen locomotives. He hurried Eva into a room the size of a soccer field, past rows of machines so huge that they made the women working at them look like dolls. Dust hung in the air, turning the sunlight pale before it reached halfway from the windows across the room. It gave the place a feeling of perpetual twilight.

After a minute Herr Schmidt stopped to talk to a dark-eyed girl whom Eva remembered from the food line that morning. Then he turned back to Eva.

"I'll get a machine ready for you," Herr Schmidt told Eva, bending low and speaking very loudly to be heard. "In the meantime Hannah will teach you what you need to know. Your sister told me you're a hard worker," he added. "I hope she's right." He nodded and walked off.

Eva started at this second reference to her sister, but Hannah began to speak at once.

"Did you bring a kerchief?" Hannah asked Eva, talking close to her ear.

Eva nodded and unfolded her kerchief reluctantly; she had wrapped her lunch in it, and now it smelled strongly of cheese. She looked pleadingly at Hannah, but Hannah told her to put it on.

"Without a kerchief your hair will be full of dust in an hour," Hannah said. "Worse, it could get caught in the machines."

Hannah helped Eva to tie the kerchief so that her hair was completely covered. After that, she turned the machine off and took Eva around to the back where a row of waist-high barrels stood on the floor.

Hannah showed Eva how a soft ribbon of combed flax was pulled up from the center of each barrel and wound around a wooden wheel at the top of the machine. From there the ribbon was spun together with another one to make a double strand of linen thread, that was wound onto a wooden bobbin. Every bobbin was as long as Eva's forearm. The whole machine was big enough to fill her bedroom on Zawale Street, Eva figured, from wall to wall and floor to ceiling.

"There are sixty barrels and thirty bobbins," Hannah told her as they came back to the front. "It's our job to get new barrels when the flax runs out and to put on new bobbins when the old ones are full. That can happen several times a day. The rest of the time we have to keep the machine running smoothly."

Hannah turned the machine on again, and instantly all the wheels, bobbins, and belts whirled into motion with a sound like a burst of thunder. Then Hannah grabbed a metal hook

56

firmly in her left hand and showed Eva how to clean lint off the axle between the wheels. "You have to do this constantly," she cautioned Eva, "or the whole machine will jam."

As she continued to clean the axle with her left hand, Hannah reached up to the top row with her right hand to reset one of the flax ribbons that had slipped off its track, then bent suddenly to clean the steel main-wheel near the floor. Eva watched in horror as Hannah's hands darted in and out of the machinery, which spun in a continuous blur, and she dreaded the moment when Hannah would hand the tools over to her.

That moment came too soon.

"For now, just try cleaning the axle," Hannah advised. "I'll show you the rest once you've gotten used to that." Eva's left hand shook so badly when she tried to reach between the wheels that she had to use both hands to steady her grip on the cleaning hook. After several attempts she managed to remove a small piece of lint. A minute later she got another piece. By the time she had cleaned the space between the first five wheels, she felt too shaky to go on.

"Just a short break," she pleaded, but Hannah pressed her to keep going.

"You can't stop, and you can't let your mind wander, no matter what," Hannah warned.

After a while Eva grew more adept at cleaning the axle and began to work with one hand. Then Hannah taught her how to reset a ribbon of flax that had fallen off its track, and how to repair a broken thread with a weaver's knot.

It was important to join the broken ends in a smooth, nearly invisible knot, she told Eva, so there wouldn't be a bump in the finished yarn. Eva had often tied knots like these when she knitted, but it was a different matter trying to tie one high over her head with machinery spinning only centimeters away from her face and fingers. Eva reached as high as she could, but she was shorter than Hannah and had to stand on her toes, making it harder to keep her hands steady.

"Watch out!" Hannah shouted, pulling Eva back by the shoulders. "Don't lean so far forward."

Eva reached up and tried again. She had nearly succeeded in tying a knot when Hannah touched her arm. "Guards," she said.

Eva looked up and dropped the ends of the thread. Two guards were walking toward her.

"Keep going," Hannah urged. She kept a hand on Eva's arm to steady her.

Eva forced herself to concentrate on tying the torn ends together. When she finished, the guards had passed and were walking away. Eva let out a long breath.

"They come through every fifteen minutes or so," Hannah told her. "As long as you keep working and fill the daily quota of bobbins, you'll be all right."

For several hours, Eva practiced what she had learned while Hannah stayed by her side every minute, helping and fixing mistakes. As the morning wore on, Eva overcame some of her fear and began to work more efficiently. Soon she was pacing quickly along the front of the machine, reaching in to clean the axle or stretching to fix a thread almost as well as Hannah. Herr Schmidt stopped by to watch her and seemed pleased with her progress; he told her that she would start working on her own machine after the lunch break.

Eva's head throbbed as she struggled to focus, hour after hour, on the tiny threads and whirring parts. She hurried without a break from one end of the huge machine to the other, but the lint accumulated on the axle as fast as she could clean it, and there seemed to be no end to broken threads, ribbons that fell off their tracks, or bobbins that needed replacing. Her throat felt sore from breathing the lint-filled air, and her legs and back ached. The large clock on the wall only said eleven o'clock; Rachel had told her that they would work until six in the evening. How would she get through a whole day of this?

Once, when she was reaching down to pick some lint off the axle, she forgot that she was still holding a rag she'd used to clean some grime off the main wheel. Before she knew what was happening, a bobbin sucked the rag from her grasp. Instantly, the bobbin jammed, and the whole machine began to vibrate, screeching like a person in pain. Hannah raced to turn off the motor, then wrestled with the rag, which had wound itself around the bobbin.

"I need to sit down," Eva pleaded, fighting tears. "Just a small break — five minutes."

"Not until lunch," Hannah replied with an alarmed glance

at Eva. She tugged out the last bit of the rag and started the machine once more. "Not even for *one* minute," she called over the roar of the motor. "The guards would see you."

At twelve o'clock a siren blared loudly, and the workers turned off their machines. Eva's ears rang in the unfamiliar silence. The room had become very hot. Her dress was damp with sweat, and her skin prickled from the lint that stuck to it. She and Hannah brushed lint from their clothes with a straw brush, then sat down on stools to eat.

"Has anyone ever lost a finger in one of these machines?" Eva asked as she chewed her bread. Her mouth was so dry that she could barely swallow it.

"Yes, but you can't think about that." Hannah took off her kerchief to shake out her short, curly black hair. "You won't feel as frightened once you get used to the work. The main thing is to keep your mind on what you're doing."

Hannah stood and brushed the lint off her bare arms. "You're lucky," she told Eva. "Everyone wants to work in this department. Herr Schmidt is kind to us, while some of the other managers —" she broke off with a shrug.

Hannah took Eva to the washroom, where they drank from a faucet and washed their faces and hands. "I look like an old peasant in this kerchief," Eva said, pulling her kerchief off with a frown. She shook her hair out, then combed it with her fingers and wound some of it into a loose roll above her forehead.

"You're still new," Hannah said, watching her with mild impatience. "After a while you'll stop worrying about how you look."

That won't happen, no matter how long I'm forced to stay here, Eva promised herself, but she didn't say anything to Hannah. She pinned the roll of hair into place with a few hairpins, then made a smaller roll right behind the first one. It was a style she'd seen in a photograph in the window of a hairdresser's shop in Bedzin several months earlier. "Springtime in Paris," the caption under the photograph had said. It had made Eva think of wide boulevards lined with dress shops and bookstalls, men and women chatting in outdoor cafés.

"I know what you're thinking," Hannah said calmly, "that they can't take your pride, or your faith, or any of what's inside you. I used to tell myself that when I first got here. Then one morning — after you've been here for a year or two, you'll see — you'll wake up and realize all of that's gone." She paused as two Czech girls entered the room, then went on. "Only by then you won't care anymore."

Eva raised her chin firmly as she tied her kerchief on again, but farther back, so that the rolls of hair were left showing at the front.

"Ten minutes until we go back to work," Hannah said in a flat, resigned voice, and started to leave.

Eva quickly straightened her dress and followed Hannah out, then across the spinning room to the furnace, which was turned off for the summer. In a dark corner behind the furnace was a bench where the girls could lie down if they were too sick to work. It was perfectly safe, Hannah assured Eva. The guards never looked there, and the Czech workers hated the Nazis so they were sympathetic to the Jews.

"What about Herr Schmidt?" Eva asked.

"He's the one who put the bench there."

They started back across the huge room, past two Jewish girls who were engaged in a heated discussion with Herr Schmidt. Books lay open on stools before them, and they all seemed to be talking at once. "That's Genia and Tzipora Gelfer," Hannah told her. "Their father was a rabbi in Kraków, and raised them as if they were going to be rabbis, too. They study Torah with Herr Schmidt nearly every lunch break."

"How can a Nazi study Torah?"

"Herr Schmidt is a devout Christian," Hannah replied. "When I first arrived he told me that he believes God sent him here to help us."

"But he's a Nazi! He said *'Heil Hitler'* in the employment office."

"He does that for the guards," Hannah said, "but here in the department it's a different story. Whenever a Jewish girl is sick, he arranges for the rest of us to take turns running her machine so she won't fall behind her daily quota of bobbins. Often he takes a turn himself."

The world had turned upside down, Eva thought as she and Hannah made their way past the rows of machines. Here was Herr Schmidt, a German who helped Jews, while Bella, a Jew, would hand another Jew over to Frau Hawlik for an extra piece of bread.

"Is the washing room in this building?" Eva asked as they passed the door to the stairway. "My sister Rachel works there."

"The washing room is down two floors, but there's not enough time to visit your sister," Hannah replied. "Is Rachel the thin one with reddish hair? Later on she'll come here to collect our finished bobbins. Maybe you'll see her then."

After the lunch break, Herr Schmidt took Eva to her own machine, which was on the opposite side of the room from Hannah's. Most of the women and girls working in this part of the room were Czech. Herr Schmidt introduced Eva to a tall blond woman named Katerina, who worked at the machine beside hers. Katerina greeted Eva with a bright smile, but Herr Schmidt reminded them that Czechs and Jews were not allowed to talk to one another and would be punished if the guards caught them. Eva could only talk to Katerina about a problem with her machine, nothing more.

After lunch there were no breaks. The room became stifling. Eva took off her shoes and worked barefoot on the concrete floor to relieve her pinched toes, but her legs and back continued to ache, and by midafternoon she began to feel that she could not stand up another minute.

Beside her, Katerina seemed untroubled by the long hours or difficulty of the work. She sang continuously, and her long, brightly colored skirt swung back and forth as she paced briskly in front of her machine, reaching out to clean the axle or fix threads with graceful sweeps of her long arms. Once, Eva recognized a song she had learned as a child and joined in, even though Katerina sang the words in Czech. *If we can't talk together, we can still sing,* Eva thought, and exchanged a quick smile with Katerina.

Late in the afternoon, Rachel came into the spinning room to collect the finished bobbins from wooden boxes placed around the room. She was coughing when she set down her load near Eva's machine.

"You have a fever," Eva said, studying her sister's flushed face.

"I'm a little tired, that's all. The lint in this room always bothers my throat." She kissed Eva on the cheek, then lifted her load of bobbins and hurried off.

At five o'clock the siren sounded for the Czech women to stop work, and Katerina prepared to leave. On her way out she took an apple and a piece of cheese from a cloth bag, and — with a quick, bright smile at Eva — left them on Eva's stool. Eva stared at her, too surprised to respond; but after she'd gone, Eva quickly hid the food in her sweater and put it under her stool. She hadn't had an apple since last Rosh Hashanah, nine months ago, when Papa had traded their last porcelain bowl for two apples.

Eva couldn't help but envy Katerina, who still had plenty to eat, and went home to her family at the end of every day. No wonder Katerina had so much energy, she thought; the Czech girl was already resting from the day, while Eva and the other Jewish girls had another hour of work, plus several more of walking or standing before they could relax. But Eva was grateful to Katerina, too, and passed the last hour of work happily imagining Rachel's surprise when she gave her Katerina's gift later that night.

At six o'clock the siren sounded for the Jewish workers to stop. Every muscle in Eva's body protested when she bent to put her shoes back on her blistered feet. She pushed Katerina's gift into the sleeve of her sweater and hurried out to the main gates, where Rachel, Kayla, Dora, and Rosie were waiting.

"I overheard two Czech girls talking in the washroom today," Dora whispered excitedly as soon as Eva joined them. Dora looked around, then continued, "They said the Soviet army is driving the Germans out of Russia! They've won battles in Kiev and all over Ukraine."

"*Raus! Raus!* Hurry!" shouted the guards, prodding the girls as they marched up and down the line.

"Kiev! That's only about a week from here by train," Rachel whispered, then fell silent as a guard went by, counting the prisoners.

"With airplanes they could be here in a few hours," Dora said once the guard had passed. "We'll be able to go home," she added, hugging Rosie.

"It might only be a rumor," Kayla cautioned. "It's best not to put too much faith in it."

But none of them wanted to believe it was a rumor. On the walk back to the train station they argued about what route the Soviet army would take, whether the soldiers would come by land or air, and how many days it would be until they reached Parschnitz. The girls began to talk of returning to their homes and families. Dora's news had lifted their spirits like the first warm wind of spring, and they spoke of nothing else all the way back.

N I N E

FOR DAYS AFTER Dora's news Eva waited, hoping to hear more reports or the sounds of distant fighting. Days became weeks. By mid-August a dusting of new snow appeared on the mountain peaks. In September, when Eva scanned the horizon for Soviet planes, she saw only flocks of birds heading south for the winter. But Dora held to her story, and embellished it, adding new reports to the first one.

"The Soviet troops were slowed down crossing the mountains," Dora announced as the girls played cards in the barracks one Sunday in October. "But they'll be here soon; they've just captured Kiev."

"I thought the Russians already captured Kiev two months ago," said Eva from a bench nearby. Although Sunday was their one day of rest, she was working busily, knitting a scarf from scraps of yarn she'd picked up in the factory weaving room. She was making it for a girl who worked in the kitchen, and who had promised to pay Eva with extra bread.

"The Soviet army doesn't ride elephants, like Hannibal," Kayla added with irritation. "Why would mountains slow them down?" Kayla shuffled the cards, which were made from pieces of cardboard she'd "liberated" from the factory shipping room. "Stop dreaming, Dora," Kayla said. "You're only making it harder for yourself."

"It's no dream," Dora insisted. "Hette Rosenzweig told me, and she heard it from a Czech woman whose son is in the army."

"You remind me of the crazy old man who used to stand outside our synagogue, announcing the date on which the Messiah would arrive. Every time that the Messiah didn't arrive as scheduled, the old man would announce another date."

"What I heard is true. You can believe it or not!" Dora threw her cards on the table angrily and stood up to leave.

"When the Soviet army marches into our camp," Kayla told her, "I promise you I'll believe it."

Rosie hesitated for a minute, then got up awkwardly and followed her cousin from the table. *Kayla is right,* Eva thought as she watched them go. It was better not to set her hopes on any of the rumors that circulated through the camp.

"I'm going to take a nap," Rachel said, yawning while she rose.

"Showers first," Eva said, quickly gathering up her knitting. "You promised," she reminded Rachel, and followed her back to their bunks. They had gotten up early that morning to wait in line for hot showers, which were available only on Sundays, but by the time they had reached the front of the line, the hot water had already run out. After a lengthy argument, Eva had persuaded her sister to come back later, when the radiators were on. That way, at least they'd be able to recover from the freezing showers in a warm room.

"We'll get sick if we don't stay clean," Eva said as she put her knitting away and took out the small cake of coarse brown soap the Germans issued. She sighed. This would be the third Sunday in a row they had had to take showers in cold water.

"I'll get sick if I catch a chill," Rachel said stubbornly. "You said so yourself. Cold water won't get my hair clean, anyway." She lay down on her bunk and pulled the blanket over her.

"That's not true," Eva replied. "If you don't wash your hair you could get boils or fleas. Cold water is better than nothing."

"It isn't water; it's snow, barely melted. One degree colder and it would freeze in the pipes."

"Just today," Eva pleaded, trying to keep her irritation out of her voice. "Next Sunday we'll get in line earlier —"

"May as well get used to it," remarked Kayla, joining them and spreading out her cards on Eva's bunk for a game of solitaire. "Even if you stand in line all night you can't count on having hot water. The Germans could turn it off at any time."

"All the more reason to wash now," Eva persisted, knowing that Kayla was right.

"Just let me sleep for a while first," Rachel said. "I can't keep my eyes open any longer. I'll take a shower today, I promise."

"Before evening rations, then," Eva agreed reluctantly. She took the week's dirty clothes to one of the sinks in the hall and began to scrub her socks with furious energy. The water felt cold as ice. Kayla threw some clothes into the sink beside her and turned on the faucet at full force.

"If I tell you something, would you give me your word that you won't repeat it to anyone?" Kayla said, speaking close to Eva's ear. "Not even Rachel?"

"You have my word," Eva said uneasily.

"I've been working with Czech partisans in the shipping room at the factory," Kayla whispered.

Eva dropped her soap, retrieved it quickly, and attempted to scrub a shirt, but she barely noticed what she was doing. Kayla a partisan? For years Eva had heard stories of the partisans, courageous men and women who fought an underground war against the Nazis. In Bedzin a group of partisans had blown up a railway bridge just as a German army supply train passed over it. But Kayla was only seventeen, and a prisoner besides. How could she help the partisans?

"We treat bolts of fabric with chemicals in the shipping room, just before they're loaded onto the trains," Kayla went on. "The chemicals weaken the fabric so that it will begin to fall apart a few weeks later."

"What if you're caught?" Eva asked, horrified at the danger Kayla was exposing herself to. With numb fingers she finished scrubbing and began to rinse her clothes in the freezing water.

"They can't trace it back to us," Kayla asserted. "Many factories supply fabric to the companies that make uniforms. And by the time the fabric disintegrates it could be anywhere in Europe, on the backs of soldiers." Kayla looked around the room cautiously, then added, "I can get you transferred to the shipping room."

"No — don't do that. Please." Eva looked at Kayla in panic. "All I want to do is keep Rachel and myself alive." She wrung out her clothes and hung them over the edge of the tub.

"You could do so much more, Eva," Kayla whispered fiercely. "When I'm fighting the Nazis, I feel free again. Think about it," she added as she gathered her clean clothes and left.

Rachel napped for the rest of the morning while Eva sat on a bench in the yard, finishing the scarf she'd started earlier. Ever since August, Eva had been bartering her knitting for food or other things that she and Rachel needed. Her first trade had been with a girl who worked in the rope spinning department at the factory, who had made Eva a pair of rope sandals. Recently, as the days grew cold and winter approached, Eva had had more orders than she could manage. Her work had paid off in extra food. As a result, Rachel had begun to look a little less tired at the end of the day, and showed more energy on the walk to the factory.

"So, Bedzin, always working, even on your day off?"

Eva stood up quickly. "Yes, Frau Hawlik." Eva had not noticed the *Lagerführerin* enter the yard from a nearby doorway, accompanied by her stone-faced assistant, Fräulein Kirschlag.

"Where did you get the wool for this scarf?" asked Fräulein Kirschlag, eyeing Eva's multicolored ball of yarn suspiciously.

"I picked up scraps from the factory, Fräulein Kirschlag."

"The cold floor in my bedroom aggravates my arthritis,"

Fräulein Kirschlag said, slowly fingering the scarf. Under her cap her dark hair was slicked back like the fur of an otter, and her eyes were so black, they seemed empty, without life. "I want a rug for my bedroom," she decided.

Just then, Bella walked toward them with a guard, who pushed two girls ahead of him with his club.

"*Vorwärts!* Move along, swine!" the guard barked.

"They were stealing potatoes, Frau Hawlik," Bella announced as the group approached.

"Please, Frau Hawlik, we didn't —" one of the girls began desperately.

"Silence! Who caught them?" Frau Hawlik demanded.

The guard indicated Bella with his wooden club.

"I suspected as much. Very well, take the Jewish dog to the kitchen and throw her a bone." Frau Hawlik waited until Bella and the guard had gone, leaving the two girls behind.

"What shall we do with these thieves?" she asked the assistant commander with mild amusement.

"Send them to the East," Fräulein Kirschlag suggested.

Eva kept her eyes fixed on the ground. She had heard those words before, and knew that they meant death for the victims.

Frau Hawlik paused for a minute, considering. "They're good workers," she said at last. "Take them away and shave their heads."

"You'll make a rug for my room," Fräulein Kirschlag reminded Eva as she left. "Get the yarn from the factory, but see that it's wool. Linen isn't warm enough."

"Yes, Fräulein Kirschlag."

"Save the girls' hair," Frau Hawlik called after her assistant. "For your rug." Fräulein Kirschlag's laughter echoed among the brick buildings.

"So, Bedzin, you Jews have it pretty easy, yes?" Frau Hawlik asked Eva after the others had left. "Just do your job and everything goes as it should, yes?" Her tone was casual, almost friendly, as if she and Eva were schoolmates out for a stroll.

"Yes, Frau Hawlik." Eva shifted uneasily, and was relieved when the *Lagerführerin* turned away a moment later.

As soon as Frau Hawlik was gone Eva hurried back to the barracks, where she delivered the finished scarf to the kitchen worker, and got a loaf of bread in payment.

When Eva returned to the third floor, Rachel was still asleep, curled up with one arm over the blanket and her face half-hidden under a mass of tangled hair. Eva started at the sight of pink fever spots on her sister's cheeks. They hadn't been there when Rachel lay down two hours ago. Rachel's face was moist with sweat, but her hands were cold. Eva took them in her own and gently rubbed them. After a few moments Rachel awoke.

"A rug!" Rachel whispered sleepily when Eva told her about Fräulein Kirschlag's order. "That ought to be worth double rations for a week! It's a big job; how will you find time?"

"I'll manage."

"I'll help you collect the yarn at lunch breaks, and I can wind it into balls for you." Rachel's face grew animated as she spoke, but she showed no interest in the bread Eva gave her, insisting that she wasn't hungry. At Eva's anxious urging, she began to nibble on it halfheartedly.

"I'm sorry I slept through the laundry again," she told Eva. "I meant to wake up earlier, to help you."

"That's all right; I'm glad you had a good rest," Eva said, taking off her rope sandals to rub her chilled toes. "It's getting too cold for sandals," she told Rachel as she changed into her leather shoes. Although the camp shoemaker had repaired her shoes and made them roomier, the open-toed sandals were more comfortable in hot weather, and Eva had worn them as far into the autumn as she could.

"Ready to wash your hair now?" Eva asked when she had put her sandals away in the locker.

Rachel looked around carefully, then said in a whisper, "Why don't we wash our hair at the factory — over lunch break, in the troughs where we wash the bobbins? Think of it, Eva, the water's always warm, and there's real soap!"

Eva was quiet, considering. "Can you trust the other girls who work there?"

"They've been washing there for weeks. I never had the nerve to try it, but it's got to be better than washing in cold water. Besides, no one has ever seen a guard there during lunch break."

"What do you think?" Rachel pressed.

Eva grinned at her. "I think we'll have clean hair tomorrow." She hugged Rachel and they began to make whispered plans.

Most of the afternoon was taken up with routine Sunday

tasks. First, the prisoners swept and scrubbed the barracks, while Bella snapped at them continuously. Then they stood in line in the *Appellplatz* for two hours while the guards counted them, taking a long break to eat their dinner in front of the girls.

It was late in the afternoon when the girls returned to the barracks, and Dora came to tell Eva and Rachel that Rosie was going to sing.

Rosie had a beautiful voice, and spent part of every Sunday singing — "staying in voice," she called it. Her parents were both music teachers and had taught her to sing and play piano from an early age.

"The mayor asked her to sing at the city hall when she was ten," Dora told Eva as they settled on a bunk at one end of the room, where Rosie had already started singing. "If things had gone differently —" Dora shook her head. "Now I worry that she'll lose her voice — without proper rest, or food, outside in all weather. And the dust in the factory makes her throat sore."

"She won't lose her voice," Eva said. "You can hear how strong and sweet it is." Dora's face brightened at this.

"You're right, Eva. As soon as the war ends, we'll go back to Lodz to find our family; then we'll all move to Palestine, where Rosie will get the best teacher. She'll be a great singer someday."

Other girls brought knitting or sewing and gathered on bunks nearby, joining in when they knew Rosie's songs. Many of them were using wire knitting needles made by the prisoners who worked in an electric plant near the spinning mill.

Rosie sang folk songs in many languages, Yiddish love songs

and ballads, opera arias, and lullabies. Those who could sang harmony, and many girls called out requests for their favorite songs.

Outside the window, the orange disc of the sun slowly melted into bands of gray clouds, then sank behind the hills. After the radiators were shut off everyone gathered closer, pulled blankets over their shoulders, and continued singing. They didn't stop until the siren sounded and the barracks lights were turned off.

For some time afterward, from her bunk across the quiet room, Rosie's voice could still be heard, humming softly.

T E N

KAYLA'S SECRET WEIGHED heavily on Eva from the moment she woke up the next morning. It gave Eva a kind of grim satisfaction to know that the Nazis were being sabotaged by Czech partisans in the factory. But it frightened her as well. Despite Kayla's claim that the ruined fabric couldn't be traced, Eva worried that the Nazis would find out; and when they did, they would make the Jews at the factory pay for it. *All* the Jews, not just those who worked in the shipping room.

Wedged on a bench between her sister and Kayla as the train clattered and swayed toward Trutnov, Eva recalled the

Polish partisans who had blown up the railroad bridge in Bedzin. When they were caught by the Nazis and hung in front of the town hall, many Jews in Bedzin had recited the mourner's prayer and honored the partisans as heros. It would suit Kayla to die a hero's death, Eva thought, but it would not suit her.

Which choice might keep Rachel and you alive for one more hour? Eva had promised Papa to ask herself that question, and she was sure the answer didn't lie in helping the partisans.

Eva was so preoccupied with these thoughts, and with the hair-washing plans she and Rachel had made, that she barely noticed the morning go by, and was surprised when the siren announced the beginning of lunch break. Her heart raced as she turned off her machine and ran down to the washing room, where Rachel awaited her. They had the room to themselves.

"I've nearly forgotten what warm water feels like," Eva said as she swirled her hand through the washing trough, which was raised waist-high on trestles, and wound back and forth across the long room. Spools of green thread lay in the bottom of the trough, where water poured over them in a continuous stream.

"What kind of thread is that?" Eva asked, peering into the trough. Countless tiny fibers had washed off the bobbins, making the water look faintly green.

"Who knows? Some kind of cotton, I suppose."

"If our hair turns green, it's your fault," Eva joked, then quickly handed Rachel an extra cotton shirt she'd brought as a towel and went outside to keep watch while Rachel washed.

After a few minutes Rachel came out and it was Eva's turn. Eva cleaned and dried her body first, standing close to the trough, then soaped her hair and dipped her head into the water to rinse. It felt so good, so luxurious to be warm and clean at the same time, that Eva wished she could climb right into the trough and soak for a while. With a worried glance at the clock, she hurried back into her clothes and went to get Rachel.

"My hair's getting thinner," Rachel said as they stood by a radiator to dry their hair. "At this rate I'll be bald soon."

"Your hair will grow back," Eva tried to reassure her. "When the war is over and we're home again it will grow back as thick as ever."

"Will it?" Rachel asked sadly. "Will anything be the way it used to?" She held out her thin arms. "Look at me; I look like an old woman."

"I'll be thirteen tomorrow, and I never got my period," Eva said, tears welling in her eyes. "I thought I was just late, but then I heard some of the older women at the camp say that the Nazis put something in our food to make us sterile. Ever since I was little I wanted to have babies, and now I'll never be able to."

"I should have talked to you about that long ago," Rachel said, putting her arms protectively around her sister. "When I stopped getting my period last April, Auntie Rivka told me it was because I was worrying too much and not eating enough. Dora and Rosie have stopped, too; I think almost everyone has.

"Don't cry, Eva; I'm sure that what you say is right. Everything will go back to normal when the war ends."

They stood quietly by the hot radiator, feeling the warmth creep into their bodies. The water rushing through the troughs made a sound like wind in the forest.

"What do you think Papa is doing right now?" Rachel asked. "Do you think he's all right?" She took a comb from her pocket and began to comb the tangles from Eva's damp brown hair.

"I don't know. I worry about that all the time." Eva thought for a while. "Papa has good connections," she said at last, "and he told me he had plans."

Who will take care of you?

I have plans, Chavele. Papa's answer played constantly in her head, like a song — maybe more like a prayer.

"What good are plans when they can take him in a raid any-time they want?" Rachel said.

At that both girls were silent.

Rachel twisted some of Eva's thick, wavy hair into a knot, then fastened a yarn flower that she had crocheted.

"It's a birthday present," Rachel said as Eva turned to see her reflection in the window. "I know your birthday's not until to-morrow, but I couldn't wait."

Just then the siren sounded for the end of lunch break.

"Thank you, Rachel. It's a long time since I had something pretty for my hair." Eva hugged her sister, then gathered her things and hurried back to work.

A light rain was falling when Eva left the factory at the end of the day. She knew there was something wrong the minute she saw her sister. Rachel's eyes were red and puffy, and tiny raised red spots were scattered over her cheeks and forehead.

"My head feels like it's on fire," Rachel complained. "My eyes sting, and it hurts to swallow." Instantly, Eva took off her heavy sweater and tried to drape it over Rachel's head and shoulders, but Rachel pushed her away.

"It could be influenza," Kayla said as she observed Rachel. "Except for the rash — has she had measles?"

"Maybe you should see Dr. Sokolow in the infirmary," Rosie suggested.

While they waited for the guards to count them Rachel seemed to be falling asleep on her feet; her head drooped, and her eyes were half-closed.

"Hold your head up, Rachel!" Eva whispered in alarm as a guard passed. Oh, God, what if she fainted?

The prisoners started to march.

"I need to lie down," Rachel muttered, and began to shuffle forward without opening her eyes. Eva put an arm around Rachel and tried to carry some of her weight, while Kayla supported her from the other side.

"*Raus! Raus!* Hurry!" shouted a guard just ahead.

Rachel's head bobbed up, and she opened her eyes a bit. Eva felt as if her shoulder was breaking from her sister's weight. Dora took Eva's place for a while, while Rosie relieved Kayla.

"Rachel, please, you have to keep going!" Eva begged as Rachel's head began to droop again. "I can see the mill; just a few minutes longer!"

By the time they reached the station Rachel's eyes had swollen so much that they were barely visible, and most of her face was covered with red spots. She was unable to climb onto the train by herself, so the four others lifted her on. Eva said a silent prayer of thanks that none of the guards had noticed.

Rachel slept on the train, leaning against Eva.

"I think your sister has tuberculosis," Kayla told Eva in a low voice as the train rattled toward Parschnitz.

"It's nothing like that!" Eva said at once, but her heart went cold at the mention of the wasting disease, which ate away at people's lungs until they finally suffocated. An image of Uncle Nuchem, coughing and pale, flashed into her mind. What if he had tuberculosis, and Rachel had caught it from him?

"She doesn't cough much," Eva reminded Kayla. This was almost true, she told herself. Rachel coughed mainly at night, or in the spinning room, where many of the girls coughed even more.

"Maybe," Kayla persisted, "but I've noticed how tired Rachel gets, much faster than the rest of us, and she's feverish a lot. I had an aunt who died —"

"Whatever Rachel has now, it only started today," Eva snapped at Kayla. "And it won't help her if she hears you talk like this."

When they reached the station Eva and her friends managed to revive Rachel, and to help her take a few, halting steps toward the camp. She passed out just as they reached the gates.

"What's going on there?" called a female guard, starting toward them. The girls struggled to hold Rachel's limp body upright.

Just then a truck drove past, and someone called to the guard, distracting her for a moment. Instantly, the girls lifted Rachel and carried her through the gates.

Rachel was put on a bed in the infirmary, and Eva waited for a long time in the hall until Dr. Sokolow called her in. By then Rachel's face was so swollen that Eva could hardly recognize her; her eyes were nothing but slits, and her mouth twisted strangely to one side, as if she were half-smiling. Rachel's face, neck, and ears were bright red from the rash. Dr. Sokolow finished her examination and directed her assistant to bandage Rachel's face.

"Your sister has a severe case of nettles," the doctor told Eva. "I've seen a number of cases recently, but generally the rash is on the patient's hands, not her face. Does your sister work with nettle fabric in the factory?"

Nettle fabric! Instantly Eva remembered the green bobbins in the washing troughs and the fibers floating in the water. She began to cry as she told Dr. Sokolow how Rachel and she had washed themselves at the factory.

"You're lucky, then," said the doctor, looking at Eva in surprise. "You must not be allergic to nettles."

The doctor pulled back Rachel's clothes as she spoke, revealing the same red rash on her stomach and upper arms. Rachel moaned and reached up to scratch herself. Dr. Sokolow grabbed Rachel's hands at once. "You mustn't scratch your skin," she warned her fiercely. "If you get an infection, there's nothing I can do to help you. Do you understand?"

Rachel moaned again and nodded weakly.

Dr. Sokolow gave some more instructions to her assistant, then led Eva out into the hall.

"Your sister will need two days of rest before she can go back to work," she told Eva very quietly. "The SS have been coming here more often. Rachel will be safe here tonight, but I advise that you take her somewhere else tomorrow."

Take Rachel somewhere else? Eva was too frightened to focus clearly. Where could she hide Rachel that the guards wouldn't find her at once?

Suddenly, the outside door slammed open, and a guard marched toward them. "I am looking for Eva Buchbinder," he growled.

Eva's heart pounded heavily.

"This is Eva," said Dr. Sokolow.

"Come with me," the guard ordered, and pushed Eva out the door and across the yard to Frau Hawlik's house.

E L E V E N

ICY CORDS OF fear tightened around Eva's chest as she stumbled up the steps to the front door. What did Frau Hawlik want with her? Had the *Lagerführerin* found out that Eva and Rachel had washed themselves at the factory?

The guard pushed Eva into the house, then down a hallway to a closed door. Talking and laughter spilled out, and tantalizing smells filled the hall. The guard knocked, and Frau Hawlik called for them to enter.

The *Lagerführerin* sat at the far end of a table at which men and women were eating. Some of them wore uniforms.

"Come here, Eva Buchbinder from Bedzin," Frau Hawlik said coolly, lifting a piece of sausage to her mouth.

Everyone fell silent and turned toward Eva as she approached. She began to shake from inside, more with every step, until she was afraid her legs would collapse before she reached the end of the table.

"You have a sister here — Rachel, yes?" Frau Hawlik smiled broadly at the others, enjoying Eva's discomfort and the chance to show off her power.

"Yes," Eva whispered. *She knows,* Eva thought, the blood draining from her face. *Frau Hawlik knows about everything.*

"Speak up!"

"Yes, Frau Hawlik." As Eva raised her head she caught a glimpse of the people nearest her. They were watching her, some with amusement, some with disgust plainly written on their faces. She looked down again at once.

"And your father owned a candy factory, yes?" Frau Hawlik went on. "His letters to his daughters are most cultivated," she informed the others before Eva could reply. "He writes in High German, if you can believe it, and so intelligently, you would hardly guess he was a Jew."

Letters from Papa! The *Lagerführerin*'s words hit Eva like gunshot. *Oh, dear God, don't let her do anything to Papa!*

"Did you help him in his factory?" Frau Hawlik asked, taking a sip of wine. "Do you know how to make candy?"

"Yes, Frau Hawlik."

"What kind?" Frau Hawlik set down her glass and fastened her cool blue eyes on Eva with hawklike interest.

"I helped make"— Eva drew a breath — "many kinds. Filled chocolates, chocolate-covered cherries, caramels, fruit-flavored bonbons —"

"Go on," said Frau Hawlik.

Eva closed her eyes, struggling to concentrate. "Cinnamon sticks, nougat, chocolate-covered marzipan, cough drops —"

At the last item the guests exploded into laughter. Only Frau Hawlik wasn't smiling or laughing.

"We shall see," she said with the same icy look. She gestured to a bag of sugar and two small bottles standing on a table nearby. "Can you make candy from these?" she asked Eva.

Eva read the labels on the bottles: green food coloring and peppermint extract. Her mind raced furiously. "Yes, Frau Hawlik."

"Take these supplies, and let her have free use of the kitchen," Frau Hawlik ordered the guard. She dumped out some nuts from a cut-glass bowl and handed the empty bowl to Eva. "I expect to see this bowl on my table tomorrow morning, filled with candy. Do you understand?"

"Yes, Frau Hawlik."

"Go!" Frau Hawlik signaled to the guard to take Eva away.

"*Mach schnell!* Be quick about it!" the guard barked as he pushed Eva ahead of him into the prisoners' kitchen. He set the ingredients on the counter and went out, slamming the door behind him.

Evening rations had ended some time ago, and Eva was alone in the room. The counters were clean and bare; tall iron kettles stood empty on the stove. Except for a strong odor of over-cooked cabbage, there was no sign that the kitchen had recently been used.

Please help me, God, Eva thought as she began to rummage through the tall cupboards along the walls, hoping to find other ingredients to add to the sugar. But all she found were utensils, containers of dried chicory roots, and cleaning supplies. In the storage room off the kitchen, boxes of vegetables and sacks of rye and wheat flour were lined up in neat rows. She grabbed a large potato and rinsed it at a sink, then ate it quickly while she searched the rest of the room. Within minutes she had looked in every corner.

There was only one thing Eva knew how to make with the ingredients she'd been given: the tiny square candies that she and Rachel had called "pillows." What if they were too plain, too ordinary to please Frau Hawlik?

Struggling against a sense of defeat, Eva rolled up her sleeves and set to work. First she took some beets from the storeroom and started to boil them, to make red coloring. Then she found a large, heavy copper bowl, a wooden spoon, and a flat metal pan, and placed them on the counter.

Was Frau Hawlik testing her? she wondered as she poured the sugar into the copper bowl. If Eva made candy and passed the test, would the *Lagerführerin* give them a lighter punishment for washing at the factory?

What if she failed?

Just thinking about it might make it happen, she warned herself, and she forced herself to focus on her work. She added water to the sugar until it was the consistency of wet sand, then put it on the stove and stirred as it slowly melted. During the busy season just before Christmas, she'd helped Papa make pillows in every imaginable flavor and color. Some of the candies were striped, she recalled, or had tiny sugar flowers pressed into their sides.

After the sugar had melted into a clear liquid, Eva tested it as Papa had taught her, dropping a spoonful into cold water to see if it formed a ball, then squeezing it gently with her fingers. But how hard was the ball supposed to be? She tried to remember, but the Nazis had taken away Papa's factory two years ago, and she hadn't made candy since.

Should she cook the sugar a little longer? If it cooked too long, she knew, the candy would be ruined.

Please, God, let this be right, she prayed as she poured the hot syrup into the metal pan to cool. Then she dumped it out onto the wood counter and tried to knead it, hoping to see it turn into the glistening golden mass that she remembered. But only a few lumps hardened, while the rest of it ran across the counter and threatened to spill onto the floor.

Oh, God, what had she done wrong? How could she turn this mess into candy?

Eva thought quickly. Maybe the sugar had been too dry. She brushed some stray hair from her face with a sticky hand, then scooped the mixture back in the pot, added a little water, and turned up the gas flame. With an image of Rachel's bandaged face constantly before her, she stirred furiously, willing the mixture to harden. One by one she repeated the steps: testing, pouring out the syrup, and kneading as before.

This time she felt the syrupy mix begin to harden in her hands. *Thank you, God, thank you!* She worked faster, pulling and folding, kneading until her arms ached. While the mixture was still pliable she divided it into two halves, sprinkling drops of dark red beet broth and peppermint onto the first half, and green coloring onto the other. She kneaded again until the color and flavor had spread evenly through each half.

By this time the candy was becoming too hard to handle. Using an empty bottle from the cupboard, Eva rolled the two mixtures, pink and green, into flat sheets, and quickly cut each sheet with a knife to make tiny squares. When they cooled the candies looked like tiny pillows, exactly as Eva remembered them, and smelled faintly of peppermint.

Eva began to weep, and her shoulders sagged with exhaustion and misery while she filled Frau Hawlik's bowl with the candy and began to clean the pots and counter. Just because Eva had made candy didn't mean she had passed the test. There was no telling how Frau Hawlik would respond; and what would happen to her and Rachel if the *Lagerführerin* didn't like the candy?

The clock above the stove pointed to two when Eva went outside to tell the guard she was done. He was huddled under the eaves, half-asleep, but he straightened quickly at her approach.

"Haven't you finished yet?" he growled.

Eva showed him the bowl, heaped with pink and green candies, and his expression changed at once.

"I'll take care of it," he said, taking the bowl, then escorting her to the barracks.

Eva looked over at the dark windows of the infirmary as they crossed the yard. What if the doctor was wrong; what if Rachel's nettles healed overnight, and she was well enough to work the next morning? *Please, God, let her get better fast.* Eva stumbled up the stairs of the barracks, dropped onto her bunk without bothering to change out of her dress, and fell asleep immediately.

She awoke the minute the lights went on the next morning, and hurried, terrified, to the infirmary. When she reached the room where Rachel lay, two guards stood at her bed, lifting her onto a stretcher. Rachel's face was hidden by the bandage, but her body seemed limp and lifeless. One thin arm hung down toward the floor.

No! Eva shouted inside her head as she ran toward Rachel. *Don't touch my sister!* Sharp pieces of colored light exploded all around her, as if the entire room were made of glass and had just shattered into fragments.

Then the doctor was beside Eva, holding her back. "Eva, calm down, it's not what you think!" she whispered. Rachel was being taken to the barracks, the doctor explained, where she could sleep safely all day with the women on the night shift.

"You can take care of her tonight," the doctor went on. "And tomorrow, with God's help, she'll be well enough to go back to work."

Eva watched numbly as the guards lifted the stretcher and carried it between the rows of beds. Then she started to understand: Rachel would be safe. It was a miracle — or perhaps not. She looked up at the doctor's weary face.

"Thank you," Eva whispered hoarsely.

"Do you think I have so much power?" Dr. Sokolow asked with a wry smile. "The order came from Frau Hawlik."

Eva nearly wept with relief as she hurried out from the infirmary. A guard was waiting for her outside.

"Frau Hawlik wants you to write down the ingredients for every kind of candy you can make," the guard said, and he handed Eva a small notebook.

Eva could almost feel Papa's hand strengthening hers as she wrote — molasses, corn syrup, confectioners' sugar, cocoa butter — for it was Papa who had taught her to spell the words, had taught her to read in the factory when she was five years old.

Where was Papa now? Suddenly Eva recalled that there had

been letters from Papa, and the memory brought a sharp renewal of pain.

But if he'd been able to send letters, maybe he wasn't in the ghetto anymore. Maybe he had escaped! Oh, God, if only she could see his letters.

Daybreak had not yet begun to pale the sky when Eva joined the rows of prisoners in the *Appellplatz*. She was glad that it was still dark so no one would see her put a piece of candy in her mouth.

"*Aufstellen!* Line up! *Mach schnell!* Make it fast!" The guards walked up and down the rows, prodding girls with rifles and counting them aloud: "forty-five, forty-six, forty-seven . . ."

The sweet taste of peppermint carried Eva to her home, the candy factory, and Papa. *One more hour,* Papa had said; *try to stay alive for one more hour.* If she had succeeded this time, it had been Papa's gift, and it had been God's gift, too.

"One hundred and seventy, seventy-one, seventy-two . . . ," the guards counted.

But there was someone else who had helped Eva, and the thought chilled her more than the icy wind that swept through the yard. Why had Frau Hawlik protected Rachel?

The *Lagerführerin* had favorites among the prisoners; life in the camp was much easier for girls like Bella or Frau Hawlik's maid. But what was the price of being a favorite? Eva wondered.

"Four hundred and four, four hundred and five . . ."

Sharp gusts of wind blew dead leaves and grit into the faces of the prisoners. Eva squeezed her eyes shut and held on to Rachel's yarn flower to keep it from blowing away.

Only then did Eva remember: today was her birthday. She was thirteen years old.

"Six hundred sixty-six, sixty-seven, sixty-eight . . ."

"Up, dirty pig! On your feet!" A girl had collapsed from cramps in her leg, and was beaten by a guard as she struggled to stand.

Next year, Eva promised herself, she would celebrate her birthday at home. Dora, Rosie, and Kayla would come to Bedzin by train, and they would all sleep in the living room, on feather beds. They would eat sandwiches ordered from the little café on May Third Square, and chocolate-covered cherries from Papa's factory. No one would have to lift a finger, and if they wanted to go out, they would ride in a taxi.

"Marsch!" The guards finished counting at last and shouted at the prisoners to march.

The line of cold and hungry girls lurched slowly forward, like a wounded animal. Eva hugged her arms around herself and began to walk.

T W E L V E

FEBRUARY. A BLIZZARD roared down from the mountains like a swarm of fighter planes bent on wiping out any trace of life in the valley. Angry winds blew the snow in every direction, sending a volley of pellets, half-snow, half-ice, rattling against the window of the train as it clattered and bumped over the icy tracks toward Trutnov.

Eva studied her sister's flushed face as she slept with her head against the window. Rachel had fallen asleep the minute she sat down in the warm train car, exhausted and numb from standing in the *Appellplatz* for an hour while the guards, barely able to see through the storm, counted the prisoners over and over.

Eva tried to recall the last time Rachel had seemed really healthy, and decided it had been in early October, around the time she'd gotten nettles. Rachel had recovered quickly from the nettles, but after that her health seemed to decline.

Even in her sleep Rachel's breathing sounded labored. With the winter months, Rachel's fevers had become more frequent, flaring up suddenly and tiring her quickly. At night she sometimes woke up drenched in sweat, her teeth chattering, so weak that she needed Eva's help to change out of her wet nightgown. She grew short of breath easily, and complained that her chest hurt.

What if Kayla was right? What if Rachel did have a wasting lung disease? Eva fought against her fears, reminding herself what a lung specialist in Kraków had told Papa years before: Rachel had weak lungs, nothing more. Given enough exercise and fresh air, she'd grow out of it in time, the doctor had assured them. Eva stared into the blinding eddies of snow hurtling past the window. The exercise and fresh air Rachel got now were part of the problem, she realized; they were only making Rachel sicker.

At Eva's urging she and Rachel had continued to wash themselves in the factory, since keeping clean was one of the only things they could do to fight sickness. But now they always checked first to find out what kind of fiber had been placed in the washing troughs that day.

Kayla leaned across the aisle and peered over her heavy glasses at the wool vest Eva was knitting. "A lot of work for a crust of bread," she commented coolly. "You could use your strength for bigger things than knitting," she added, but Eva shook her head. Didn't Kayla understand she wasn't interested in risking her neck for the partisans?

"How long would it take you to make me a thick hat like Rachel's?" Kayla asked, abruptly dropping her critical tone.

"Not long, but I've already got more requests than I can

handle for the next three weeks," Eva said, smiling at Kayla's sudden interest in her knitting.

"I could get the yarn for you," Kayla offered.

"You'll have to anyway," Eva told her. "I don't have time to collect it anymore." That was the one good thing about winter: the cold weather had kept her knitting business strong. Eva's customers included not only other prisoners, but also Czech women at the factory, friends of Katerina. By working nearly every spare minute, sometimes late into the night, Eva had been able to bring in a small but steady supply of extra rations. Adding to that Katerina's occasional gifts of a turnip or potato, Eva and Rachel were better off than most of the others. But it was not enough; one look at her sister's pale, thin face reminded Eva of that.

She was still thinking about this, and wondering what more she could do, when a girl squeezed onto the bench beside her and began to talk. "Please, I need your help," the girl pleaded. "It's my stomach — I have terrible diarrhea, but the doctor has no medicine. Sometimes the cramps are so bad, I can't stand up."

"Why do you ask me?" Eva said uncomfortably.

"Everyone knows you're one of Frau Hawlik's favorites," the girl begged. Her eyes were ringed with dark circles, as if she hadn't been sleeping.

"I'm sorry," Eva said, drawing back in surprise. "I wish I could help, but I have no — no power —"

"But you make candy for her; you made a rug for Fräulein Kirschlag. And they helped your sister when she was sick."

She thinks I'm like Bella, Eva realized in discomfort, and tried to explain that even though she had made candy for Frau Hawlik several times, she had no more influence over the *Lagerführerin* than any other prisoner. And although it had taken Eva and Rachel two weeks to collect enough yarn for Fräulein Kirschlag's rug, then three weeks more to crochet it, working long into the nights, the assistant commander hadn't given them so much as a crust of bread for their trouble.

"Please, I'm desperate," the sick girl persisted. "If you would only talk to Frau Hawlik or Fräulein Kirschlag —"

The train whistled to signal its arrival at the Trutnov station.

"I'm sorry," Eva said again as the train slowed, and she turned to wake Rachel.

An icy blast of wind lashed the girls the second they stepped off the train. Eva had sewn a thick lining of unspun cotton into Rachel's coat and had lengthened her own heavy sweater into a coat, but the garments were no match for the glacial wind or the masses of snow it hurled at them.

Eva and Rachel quickly locked arms with Dora, Rosie, and Kayla, and pressed their bodies tightly together as they started the long walk to the factory. Eva ducked her head to keep the snow from pelting her face. She was barely able to draw a breath without inhaling a mouthful of snow, and every gasp of frozen air cut her lungs like a knife.

The snow didn't seem to fall, but blew up, sideways, every direction but down. Snow melted, then froze on Eva's face, and melted on her tongue with a taste like metal. Wind scalded her nose and the tips of her ears painfully, and a layer of ice formed on her eyelashes so that she could barely blink. Whenever she raised her head it was only to squint into a white whirlwind, or the snow-covered shapes of girls just ahead. Ghostly images of trees occasionally sprang up from the blinding blizzard, and Eva struggled to identify a landmark that would tell her how far they had come, how far they had to go. But it was like looking into the foaming rapids of the river; like staring into white darkness.

"Are you all right?" Eva shouted in Rachel's ear. In answer, Rachel pressed Eva's arm with her own.

Then Kayla called something to Eva, but her voice was lost in the howling wind.

"What?" Eva shouted back.

"Nice day!" Kayla repeated.

Eva tried to nod, but her scarf and collar had frozen solid as a vise, making it impossible to move her head. She felt as if her hands and feet had frozen, too, that she was marching along on unbending blocks of ice.

After that no one spoke until they reached the factory, where they unlocked their frozen arms and hurried into the warm buildings as quickly as they could.

Eva stripped off her shoes and wet woolen stockings the moment she reached her machine and hung her stockings to dry in the washroom. She put on the extra pair she had carried in her pocket, then set her shoes by the furnace to dry out. Other girls joined her, spreading wet clothes and shoes wherever they could.

Many of the girls in the spinning room, especially the Jewish workers, had developed chronic coughs, red, teary eyes, and gravelly voices. Their sneezing and coughing echoed across the huge room. Then it was time to start work, and all other sounds were lost under the whirr and clatter of machinery and the roar of motors. Katerina still had enough energy to sing as she worked, but Eva could barely keep up with her tasks, and she didn't join in the songs.

By midday break Eva's shoes had dried, and she had put them on again. She had just finished her lunch of bread and cheese and was drinking water at the sink when Katerina and two other Czech girls entered the washroom. They washed their faces, straightened their hair, and used the toilets, talking to each other the whole time in rapid Czech. Eva understood almost none of the words, until one of the girls mentioned the names of some towns in Poland. Bedzin was one of the towns.

"What did she say about Bedzin?" Eva demanded of Katerina in German. Instantly the Czech girls stopped talking.

"She has relatives in Poland," Katerina began hesitantly. "They hear reports of the war."

"I'm from Bedzin!" Eva's voice rose. "Tell me!" she nearly shouted.

"Mother of God," Katerina said, tears welling in her eyes. "I'm sorry. My friend heard that the Germans have rounded up everyone in the Bedzin ghetto — and sent them to a camp in Auschwitz."

Eva felt as if all the air had been sucked from the room. She stood facing Katerina as if she was still waiting for the Czech girl to speak. No one moved.

Katerina was first to break the silence: "Eva, this is only something my friend heard. It may not be true. We don't know what to trust — what to believe anymore."

"It's a rumor, isn't it? Isn't it?" Eva repeated in a louder voice. She felt cold all over.

"Maybe, yes. As you say, a rumor."

The siren blew to signal the end of lunch break. Silently the Czech girls filed from the room, all except Katerina. She touched Eva on the arm.

Eva started and looked up at Katerina in surprise, as if she didn't know how she had gotten there.

"The siren —" Katerina faltered. "It's time to go back to work."

Katerina took Eva's hand and led her back to their machines. She pulled the wooden bar to start Eva's machine, then put the cleaning tool in Eva's hand and said something close to her ear, but Eva didn't understand.

Why was Katerina upset? Where was Papa? Something was terribly wrong. She needed Papa to help her, to comfort her, to tell her what to do. Papa would know.

"Get to work!" Katerina began shouting in German. She grabbed Eva hard by the shoulders and shook her. "A guard will see you!"

Eva trembled and stared into the moving machinery as if it weren't there. *Oh, God, what has happened to Papa? Don't let him be taken; don't let it happen!*

"Snap out of it!" Katerina yelled, then suddenly disappeared from Eva's side.

"What's this?" shouted a guard, stepping close to her machine. "Why are so many bobbins not turning? Have you been asleep, lazy swine?"

Eva came alive at once and raced to fix the broken threads, but she could not make her hands stop shaking, and half of the knots came undone as soon as she tied them. New threads seemed to break faster than she could fix the old ones.

Papa, Papa! Where are you?

"Disgusting, lazy piece of filth!" The guard raised his club threateningly and swore at Eva in German.

Just then Katerina arrived with Herr Schmidt.

"Thank you for trying to fix this broken machine," Herr Schmidt shouted to Eva. "You may go back to your own machine now." He pushed Eva gently in the direction of Katerina's machine.

"I'll have to take the motor apart again," Herr Schmidt said, directing his words to the guard as he quickly shut off Eva's machine. "The oil we've been getting lately is ruining all the motors."

"We're having the same problem with the trucks," said the guard, changing his tone immediately.

Katerina kept Eva busy at her machine while the guard remained talking with Herr Schmidt. As soon as the guard left, Herr Schmidt came over and took Eva's cleaning hook from her hand.

"Go and rest awhile," he said gently, mopping his face with his handkerchief. "Katerina and I will watch your machine."

Eva curled up on the bench behind the furnace for a long time, her thoughts racing feverishly. Papa had plans, she told herself over and over. He had plans and good connections. Even if the Nazis had deported the entire ghetto — and she fought fiercely against believing it — they might still have kept Papa there to work at the construction depot. Or Polish partisans might have smuggled him out. She had heard stories of Jews who were allowed to hide in a farmer's barn in exchange for work.

But a voice inside her said that Papa had not escaped. And what of Auntie Rivka, Uncle Nuchem, little David? Her heart felt as if it would burst against her ribs. She felt more lost and frightened than ever.

Oh, God, how could she tell Rachel? She had to tell her; Rachel was Papa's daughter, too. But what if the news made her sicker?

What if the news wasn't news at all, but only a rumor? Why worry Rachel for nothing?

"Don't give your worries any power," Auntie Rivka used to say when Eva was little. "You might make them real."

But even if she didn't say anything, how could she hide her thoughts from Rachel? Surely Rachel would read Eva's fear in her face.

Eva closed her eyes and prayed for sleep, but sleep didn't come. Instead she saw an image of Papa, so alive that she nearly cried out. Not gray and bent, as she had last seen him, but strong and full of laughter, pulling her and Rachel on a sled along the frozen river in Bedzin.

Eva buried her head in her arms and sobbed. *Don't leave me, Papa,* she begged silently. She grasped the narrow wooden bench with her hands and cried as if she would never stop.

Finally, exhausted, she went to wash her face at the sink, then looked out the washroom window. Past the factory buildings lay the river, and beyond the river the hills rose, white and still. It was no longer snowing, but the sky was overcast with gray clouds, promising another storm. In the west the clouds were streaked with crimson, as if heaven were bleeding. A flock of birds lifted above the hills. They wheeled suddenly, flew into a bank of clouds, and were gone.

"Papa, please be alive," Eva said to the sky.

PART II

September 1944–May 1945

T H I R T E E N

THE LONG WINTER was over at last in April, followed by a brief, rainy summer that marked the end of Eva's first year in the camp. The only sign of hope for the prisoners was that the return of warm weather brought some relief from sickness. In June Rachel's high fevers and cough began to subside noticeably, and often disappeared for days a time. But by September the days grew shorter and cooler once more, and Eva started to brace herself for another winter.

Yom Kippur, at the beginning of the Jewish New Year, fell on the twenty-sixth of September. The holiday, the holiest day of the Jewish calendar, began at sundown as the prisoners were leaving the factory. From the minute they began to march toward the Trutnov station they argued about whether to observe the traditional daylong Yom Kippur fast.

"The Torah commands us to fast, to purify our souls for the New Year," one girl announced, as if that settled the matter.

"We're fasting every day as it is," Kayla replied. Several girls agreed loudly.

"It was different last year, when we had more to eat," Dora pointed out. "At least we could fill our stomachs at the end of the fast." No one argued with this. In the past year the bread ration had gotten steadily smaller, and so tough that it was barely edible. A rumor spread in the camp that the flour was mixed with sawdust; some girls even claimed to have seen bags of sawdust delivered to the kitchen. Now cheese was seldom given out anymore, and the cabbage in the soup was rotten, making the broth sour.

"No matter what, we should fast to honor God!" cried a girl whose father had been principal of a religious school.

"What's God doing for us?" Kayla snapped back at her.

"She's right! Where is God, that these things happen to us?" cried another girl.

"How can you talk like this?" The principal's daughter was crying now.

"Perhaps we could give up only half of our rations," suggested a round-cheeked girl nearby.

"Some sacrifice," Rosie muttered. "You get potatoes from your cousin in the kitchen."

"That's a lie! She never gave me a crumb!"

Sharp pangs of hunger tormented Eva as she listened to the debate. Her sources of extra food had all but disappeared in the last half-year. None of the prisoners could afford to give up any rations to pay for Eva's knitting. Even the Czech girls seemed to have less to eat, and Katerina rarely left gifts of food for Eva anymore.

Still, Eva had made up her mind to fast again this year.

"Papa wouldn't expect you to fast," Rachel reminded her gently. "The Talmud exempts those who are ill or starving."

"I know."

"Then why?"

Eva sighed. How could she explain without saying more than she should, without revealing what she'd heard, months ago, about the Bedzin ghetto? How could Rachel understand what Eva allowed herself to believe: that if she found the strength to complete the fast, some of that strength might pass, through some mysterious process, to Papa? It didn't make sense, Eva knew, but she still held on to the hope.

Rachel and Kayla tried to talk her out of her decision all the way back to camp, while they waited in the food line, and in the barracks, where Eva stored her uneaten dinner in her locker.

"You're crazy," Kayla told her outright. "We're already starving."

"What if you faint?" Rachel pressed her.

"I'll carry my food to the factory," Eva told them. "If I start to feel faint I'll eat some of it," she insisted, and finally Rachel and Kayla stopped trying to persuade her.

The next morning as they walked from the Trutnov station to the factory, Eva carried her bread in her pocket and her bowl of soup in her hands, grasping the metal lid tightly so that none of the soup would spill out.

It was a beautiful autumn morning, and the yellow leaves of the old chestnut trees along the walkway trembled above the girls like Japanese fans. Dora and Rosie reminisced about their school in Lodz, the courses and teachers they had liked best, but Eva barely paid attention. Hunger gnawed at her as she marched, and it was all she could do not to lift the lid and drain her soup in one gulp. How would she make it to the end of the day?

"You could use your strength for bigger things," Kayla told Eva once more as they parted by the gates. "There's still time to join us," she whispered amid the confusion of people hurrying into the factory. "You can choose, Eva — you are free to do so."

"I do choose." Eva's back stiffened, and she held tightly to her bowl as she faced Kayla.

"I'd expected you to show more sense." Kayla frowned disapprovingly when they parted for the day.

Herr Schmidt called a meeting of the workers in his department as soon as they had all arrived.

"Today is the day for our annual cleaning of the machines," he announced. "Leave the motors off, and take time to clean every part thoroughly, especially those parts that you can't reach when the machine is operating.

"I have already informed the guards that today is a special cleaning day, so they won't expect you to do any spinning, but keep in mind that they will be coming through to inspect as usual."

Eva smiled at Hannah as they listened. Since the workers kept their machines free of lint every day, there would be little for them to do today except look busy whenever the guards came through. Herr Schmidt never once mentioned Yom Kippur, but the Jewish girls knew that he was aware of the holiday, and had discussed it beforehand with Genia and Tzipora, the rabbi's daughters. He had done the same thing last year, scheduling a cleaning day on Yom Kippur so that the Jewish girls would be free to pray and rest for most of the day.

As they had done the year before, Eva and Katerina agreed to take turns watching for guards. Eva had brought her books of prayers and psalms, and read them whenever she was free. While she chanted the prayers silently she saw once more the high, domed ceiling of the great synagogue in Bedzin where she had sat in the women's balcony between Rachel and Auntie Rivka. Eva had loved the way the stained-glass windows threw patches of amber, red, and purple onto the white prayer shawls of the men standing below. One of the prayers spoke of standing in God's holy light, and as a child she had thought this is what the prayer had meant.

Inscribe us for another year in the book of life, Eva read in Hebrew. What would God write in His book beside her name, she wondered. Stubborn? Proud? She was both, she knew. Hardworking; she was that, also, and she had tried to be brave.

But it wasn't enough. Winter was coming; Rachel's fevers were bound to get worse, and this year Eva had no way to get extra food.

Tears began to fall down her cheeks, and she made no effort

to stop them. *Either we will find a path around, or God will teach us how to fly.* Papa had been wrong. Sometimes there wasn't a path around. And where was God?

Eva began to lose patience with the prayers in her book, most of which either praised God or begged His forgiveness for having sinned. None of them sounded like they'd been written by people who were hungry or frightened. Finally she closed the prayer book and opened Papa's book of psalms to the first page.

> *In the path that I should take*
> *They have hidden a snare;*
> *I look to my right hand,*
> *I find no friend at my side.*
> *No way of escape is in sight,*
> *No one comes to rescue me . . .*

Eva stopped, surprised, and read the lines again. It was as if the psalmist were speaking her thoughts. She settled herself into a more comfortable position, turned the page, and continued to read.

> *I lift my eyes to the mountains;*
> *Where will my help come from?*
> *My help is from God,*
> *Creator of heaven and earth.*
> *He will not let your foot give way;*
> *Your Guardian will not slumber.*

The words comforted Eva and filled her with a sense that she had not been abandoned. She did not expect that troops of angels would fly over the mountains to Parschnitz, but she allowed herself to believe that help was on the way. If only she and Rachel could stay healthy through the winter, she thought; if only they could hold on until spring. *Inscribe us for another year.* Then, perhaps, Allied airplanes would come at last to free them.

At lunch break Rachel came to make sure that Eva wasn't in any danger of fainting. During the break Genia and Tzipora Gelfer read aloud the story of Jonah and the whale, the traditional afternoon biblical reading for Yom Kippur. Eva and Rachel joined the girls who gathered to listen as the rabbi's daughters read the Hebrew text, then translated it into Yiddish. Eva closed her eyes and let the words spill over her, carrying her home to Papa, who had told them the story every Yom Kippur when they were little. For a shattering instant Eva ached for Papa to be with her and Rachel, and for all of them to be sitting at the old wooden table in the kitchen. She opened her eyes and looked at Rachel, wondering if she was remembering the same thing.

"I hope Papa has a chance to pray today," Rachel said instead, sending Eva's thoughts reeling in another direction. "At the construction depot they often make him work so late, Yom Kippur could be over before he gets back to the ghetto."

Eva nodded, turning her head so Rachel couldn't see her face.

"Eva, what's wrong?" Rachel asked. "I wish you would eat something. You don't look well."

"It's nothing," Eva lied, and was relieved when the siren sounded, announcing the end of lunch break.

Later in the day Herr Schmidt came over to talk to Eva. "Some of the people in town have shortwave radios," he told her in a low voice. "I hear reports — trustworthy ones, I believe — from the radio, and from friends back home." Eva waited and held her breath.

"British forces have taken most of Italy, the Americans have freed France, and the Soviets are pushing the German army out of eastern Poland," Herr Schmidt went on. To her frightened look, he added, "I have no news of civilians, only of battles and air strikes, all showing that the German army is retreating back to Germany, pursued by Allied troops." He ran a hand over his bristled hair, making it stand up even straighter than before.

"There's more, much more; there isn't time to tell you everything. But the Allies are winning on every front. Many say it will all be over in a matter of weeks, perhaps even before winter. I thought you would like to know this."

"Thank you; yes, it's wonderful news —" Eva said. Herr Schmidt looked anxious and tired. *Friends back home,* he'd said; she didn't know exactly where "home" was, but she knew he had lived in Germany until the Nazis had sent him to work in Trutnov. Perhaps he had a wife and children; if so, who knew what danger they might be in? "Thank you for telling me," she said respectfully.

Afraid to let herself hope but unable to stop herself, and weak with hunger, Eva sat down and cried for several minutes after Herr Schmidt left. *Thank you, God,* she thought over and over. It was all she could do to keep from running downstairs to tell Rachel.

The sun was setting as Eva left the factory. Yom Kippur was almost over. She was tired and painfully hungry, but proud that she had completed the fast, and strengthened with new hope. Dora, Rachel, and Rosie were waiting by the gates as usual. Eva lost no time in sharing Herr Schmidt's report.

"What have I been telling you?" Dora was jubilant and immediately added some new items from her store of gossip. Recently hundreds of girls from Hungary had arrived in the camp, bringing with them firsthand accounts of the war. Dora had befriended several Hungarian girls and seemed to have new stories every day.

Rosie and Rachel listened to all of this with trembling emotion, unsure what to believe.

Eva understood their hesitation. "I don't think Herr Schmidt would say anything unless he was sure of his source," Eva tried to reassure them.

"Free by winter," Rachel said slowly, as if she were tasting something sweet with the words. "It seems too good to be real."

"Five to a row! *Schnell!* Quickly!" The guards began their evening count of the prisoners.

"Where's Kayla?" Dora asked. It wasn't like her to be late.

The friends compared notes; no one had seen Kayla since they had parted in the morning.

"*Achtung!* Attention!" the guards called suddenly, stopping in the middle of their count. "Silence!"

Frau Hawlik stepped forward from a nearby building and began to address the prisoners.

"Five Jewish workers disappeared today," she announced angrily. "They could not have done so without help."

No one moved while the *Lagerführerin* walked along the line of prisoners, watching their faces. A cool breeze blew up from the river, making Eva shiver.

"Very well, then!" Frau Hawlik shouted angrily when she'd reached the end of the line. "Make no mistake: we shall find these enemies of the Reich — those who escaped, and those who helped. All will be caught! All will be killed!" She raised her fist as she shouted, then turned abruptly and left.

Instantly, the guards shouted for the prisoners to march. Eva, Dora, Rosie, and Rachel walked in silence; a fifth girl joined them, taking Kayla's place. As they passed the river Eva looked across it, toward the hills, and prayed that her friend would make it to safety. *I lift my eyes to the mountains; where will my help come from?*

For a moment Eva felt a twinge of regret, remembering how Kayla had urged her to join the partisans. If she had gone with Kayla she might be free now. But the feeling didn't last. Rachel would never survive a winter living in the forests, she reminded herself; to join Kayla, Eva would have had to leave Rachel.

"Eva, look." Rachel pointed high above the hills, where the first stars glowed faintly in the darkening sky. Yom Kippur was over. Eva immediately took her dry bread from her pocket and began to chew it, taking careful, small sips from her bowl of soup. She felt light-headed, but whether it was from hunger or the unexpected prospects of freedom she'd glimpsed that afternoon, she couldn't tell.

"To break the fast," Rachel said, slipping something into Eva's pocket.

An apple! Memories wrapped around Eva like a shawl as she felt the fruit, cool and firm, in her pocket. Papa had always given them apples dipped in honey at the close of Yom Kippur. "For a sweet year," he would say.

"I wish we had honey," Rachel said. Then, very softly, "I wish we had Papa."

The sound of the river traveled through the trees, as quiet as breathing. In the twilight Rachel's face was suffused with the old pain and worry, and the new hope, all at once. Eva's eyes filled; she squeezed Rachel's hand silently.

"For a sweet year," Rachel whispered.

F O U R T E E N

A STORM GATHERED over the camp, moving quickly from the east. Swift-flying clouds wheeled drunkenly across the sky, where stars glittered like fragments of broken glass. The stars provided the only light shining on the *Appellplatz,* where the prisoners had just returned from the factory, and waited in the intense cold for the guards to finish their count. Eva could barely see the features of girls just ahead of her. For months, by Nazi government order, every street lamp in Trutnov and Parschnitz had been kept off, and every window heavily curtained, to prevent the towns from being spotted at night by Allied aircraft.

Snow began to fall in wet flakes that covered the girls' heads and shoulders. Rachel had been sneezing and coughing ever since they left the factory; she held her mittened hands over her mouth to stifle the sound. Eva drew closer and put her arm around her sister. Now would be a good time for the Allies to arrive, she thought; *now,* before Rachel got any sicker. What had happened to the confident predictions Herr Schmidt had shared with her three months ago? What was stopping the Soviet army or other Allied forces from reaching them? *Please, God, let them come now.*

"Achtung!" a guard shouted suddenly, and other guards took up the cry. "Attention! Silence!"

Fräulein Kirschlag stepped onto a raised platform in front of the prisoners. Tension traveled through the rows of girls like an electric current.

"Everyone must be prepared to sacrifice for the Reich!" Fräulein Kirschlag shouted.

Eva tightened her hold on Rachel. What was left, that they hadn't sacrificed already?

"There will be no more trains to Trutnov, starting tomorrow!" the assistant commander announced. "To allow time for walking, rations will be distributed starting at four-thirty A.M. The day shift will line up in the *Appellplatz* at five, and leave camp at five-thirty!" Fräulein Kirschlag stepped off the platform and departed as abruptly as she had come.

For a minute afterward the prisoners stood silent, frozen in shock; then the guards shouted at them to get going, and they filed through the yard to line up for rations. A rumor spread quickly through the line that there would be double rations of bread from now on. Many believed it, maintaining that the Germans would have to feed them better, now that they had to walk all the way to Trutnov. But the rumor died the instant the girls saw their rations: a half-bowl of thin beet soup, sour-smelling and cold.

"The Germans can't even keep our little train running," said Dora as the girls ate their soup in the barracks. "Don't you see? This is good news: it shows the Germans have practically lost the war!"

"You and your good news," Eva said grimly. It was only December; at least three more months of winter lay ahead.

"A little more good news, and we'll all be dead," Rachel put in.

"In September Herr Schmidt said we'd be free by winter," Rosie reminded Eva with a hint of resentment.

"*Maybe* by winter," Eva said, tired.

"Winter has just begun," Dora reminded them. "The Allies could still come before —"

Eva left the table quickly, not wanting to hear any more, and went off to prepare for bed. Five kilometers to Trutnov, five more back: she didn't think that her bones could hold any more tiredness — her heart, either. And how would Rachel walk so far, when she had barely been able to keep up with the others as it was? Eva shivered in the cold room as she changed out of her dress.

Her nightgown was still in good condition, she noted as she slid it quickly over her head, and the lace collar looked almost new; maybe she could sell it to Bella, the *Blockalteste*, for a piece of bread. Plump, mean Bella always seemed to have plenty to eat.

Eva pulled her sweater and coat back on over her nightgown; for months the radiators in the barracks had been turned down so low that all the girls kept their coats on indoors. The coat that had fit Rachel tightly last winter now hung loose from her shoulders. Eva noticed it and made a mental note to offer her nightgown to Bella the next day.

"Several girls have had food stolen from their lockers," Rachel told Eva in a low voice. "There were some arguments at the table about who had stolen it."

Eva nodded quietly and took their bread from their lockers. "I'll keep it with me," she promised.

Most of the prisoners went to bed the moment they finished eating, too tired to talk. The lights were shut off early, leaving the room in complete darkness. Eva waited a few minutes to make sure that Rachel was asleep, then sat up in bed and unwrapped their bread, which they had covered with clean kerchiefs.

A new bread ration had been distributed that morning; it was meant to last three more days. Since the rations had been cut back to a half-loaf, Eva had taken over the exacting task of dividing the bread into equal daily portions for herself and Rachel. Now she broke off part of her own loaf and added it to Rachel's share. If she did this for the next two days, Eva calculated, she'd end up with nothing to eat on the fourth day, the last day before new rations were given out. She would have to hide the truth from Rachel — or perhaps by then Eva would be able to find another scrap of food somehow.

She wrapped the portions in their kerchiefs once more and curled up with the bread in her arms, but she couldn't fall asleep.

Every time she closed her eyes she saw tables piled with food — roast chicken, noodles with gravy, apple dumplings, all her favorite dishes. The wheaty smell of the bread began to torture her. Her mouth watered until she thought she'd have to put the bread back in the locker and take her chances on having it stolen rather than have to hold it all night.

All across the room girls moaned, coughed, muttered, or cried out in their sleep. Next to her Rachel wheezed while she slept, then suddenly broke into a cough that sounded as if it would tear her lungs from her chest. It didn't last long, and afterward Rachel began to breathe more easily, but even so Eva remained restless.

Last week Rachel had fainted at work; without warning, in the middle of the day. Instead of Rachel, another girl had come to collect the bobbins that afternoon and had stopped by Eva's machine to tell her. Rachel was all right, the girl had said; they had revived her quickly by throwing water on her from the washing troughs.

Terrified, Eva had begged Herr Schmidt to arrange that Rachel be transferred to the spinning department, but he had said that such a request would only arouse the suspicion of the Nazi authorities.

What if Rachel fainted while they were walking? Eva stared into the darkness of the room, recalling Rachel's clumsy gait as she'd walked from the factory that evening, like a puppet whose strings had become tangled. And lately Rachel had seemed distracted, inattentive, her words wandering as if she were talking in her sleep. Sometimes she'd break off halfway through a sentence, then not remember what she had been talking about.

These thoughts kept Eva awake for a long time, until finally, exhausted, she fell into a troubled sleep.

The next morning the camp yard was buried knee-deep under new snow, and more was falling. After a hurried count, the prisoners were marched out the front gates of the camp and onto the main street of Parschnitz. Snow came down heavily, and blew into the faces and down the collars of the prisoners as they struggled through snowdrifts. Eva's wool stockings were soon covered with a layer of ice; she would have given anything for a pair of the thick pants or high leather boots that the guards wore. Eva and Rachel had wrapped their scarves up to their chins, but the bitter wind scalded every inch of exposed skin and made every breath painful. The guards, furious at having to get up hours before dawn to trudge through the blizzard, swore at the prisoners and hit them with clubs and rifles, then forced them to go so fast that they were practically running.

The main street was deserted; the only sounds were the wind and the muffled thud of hundreds of pairs of wooden shoes on the snowy pavement. Eva and Rachel were among the few who still wore leather shoes. On one of the shoemaker's last visits to the camp the previous summer, he had put new soles on Eva's shoes, and Eva was determined to hold on to them as long as possible. When they wore out, she'd have no choice but to get a pair of the ill-fitting wooden shoes, which gave their wearers blisters in summer and frostbite in winter.

The guards' flashlights were all but useless in the blinding flurries, and no other lights were on to show them the way. Every house and shop along the main street was shut up tight, with not a ray of light coming through the blackout curtains.

"Will the Allied airplanes bomb our factory?" Eva had asked Herr Schmidt months earlier, when the blackout had first been imposed. "Will they bomb Trutnov or Parschnitz?"

"Oh, no, I think not," Herr Schmidt had assured her. "The Allies have targeted oil refineries, major rail lines and transportation centers, and military plants that manufacture planes or weapons. They have no interest in a textile mill or a little town in the mountains."

As they passed a bakery a flash of light startled Eva, but it was only an old woman opening the bakery door to throw a dishful of crumbs onto the snow. Immediately some tiny, dark birds swooped down out of the storm and began to peck at the crumbs. The smell of fresh-baked bread from the open door was nearly more than Eva could bear.

"The birds eat better than we do," Dora said bitterly.

Eva felt the tiny portion of bread in her pocket and counted the hours until lunch. She wished she had not given some of her ration to Rachel. Why should she eat less than her sister? Didn't she work as hard and suffer as much?

It seemed like they had been walking for hours when they passed a sign marking the boundary between Parschnitz and Trutnov. They were only halfway there. Numb with cold and struggling to keep up the pace at which the guards drove them, the prisoners dragged themselves along the dark streets.

The new snow hid a layer of ice on the pavement that made every step treacherous. Eva kept her arm locked with Rachel's and tried to steady her, but she was stumbling herself, and nearly fell several times. When they finally reached the factory Eva barely had the strength to exchange a few hurried words with Rachel before they went inside.

The minute she reached the spinning department, Eva stripped off her ice-coated stockings and shoes, then sat down in the warm corner behind the furnace to rub her feet and legs, which stung as badly as if she had been attacked by bees. As soon as she began to warm up she felt light-headed, and had to lie down on the bench.

Soon the space behind the furnace was crowded with girls who had come to warm up and rest. Many were coughing; all of them were too tired to talk.

Eva was still feeling dizzy when the siren sounded a minute later. She hauled herself to her feet and went slowly to her machine, holding on to the wall to steady herself.

Throughout the morning Eva struggled to stay alert, but the long walk had drained much of her energy, and as the hours passed, the heat and constant work continued to wear down her senses. Her eyes hurt from focusing on the whirling machinery. More than once Katerina came over to point out broken threads that Eva had not noticed.

Lord of the universe, keep Papa strong, Eva prayed whenever she tied the torn ends together. *Keep Uncle Nuchem strong; keep Auntie Rivka, and David.* But even as she prayed, another thread would break, then another. And Eva shuddered, wondering if this was God's answer.

At the midday break Eva gobbled her tiny portion of bread, but it barely softened her piercing hunger, so she went to the washroom and tried to fill her stomach with water. Before the mirror she brushed lint from her kerchief and from the rolls of brown hair that she always left uncovered, just above her face. One of the rolls had come loose and fell onto her forehead in tangled loops, but she was past caring how she looked. Without bothering to straighten her hair, she splashed some water on her face and went back to work.

As the afternoon dragged on, Eva's tiredness gave way to lethargy, then a kind of half-awake numbness, until the only part of her that seemed fully alive was her empty, raging stomach. By the time Katerina left at five o'clock Eva felt as if she couldn't stand up another minute. Without Katerina to help her focus on her work, her attention began to wander. More than once she felt her eyes close and her head drop, then she'd pull herself up with a start. It was no use trying, she reasoned sluggishly; if she didn't lie down soon, she'd fall asleep where she stood. She yawned and stretched on her toes toward the wooden lever that turned off the motor.

But just as she took hold of it, she thought she saw a broken thread hanging loose across the axle. Without thinking, Eva ducked and reached back toward the thread. Instantly a terrible pain shot through her head. She screamed and struggled to pull herself away, but the machine held her head and dragged her closer, into its whirling metal jaws. Then everything went black.

F I F T E E N

EVA TRIED TO open her eyes, but something held them shut. Her head felt as if it were on fire. Nightmarish images hovered at the edge of her consciousness: she was lying still, but moving quickly; terrible, blinding colors mixed with intense cold. Then Eva heard Rachel's voice, praying, and lifted her hand toward the sound.

"Eva!" Rachel's arms wrapped around her gently. "Thank God, thank God," she said, weeping. "You had an accident — yesterday, at the factory. Some of your hair was pulled out; do you remember?"

Involuntarily Eva moved her hand to her head, but it was covered with something, and felt much bigger than it should. Half-formed images came back to her: a broken thread; the bobbins, much too close; and a terrible pain, which was still there, throbbing in her temples, piercing through to her skull. Eva tried to speak, but her tongue felt thick and strange, and she couldn't form the words.

"Don't try to talk," Rachel said soothingly. "You're in the infirmary; you've been here since yesterday. Let me tell the doctor you're awake."

Dr. Sokolow came in and examined Eva briefly, then lifted her so she could drink some water. The pain in Eva's head grew worse when she moved her jaw, but she was terribly thirsty, and the cool water soothed her mouth and throat.

"Herr Schmidt telephoned Frau Hawlik the moment you were injured," Rachel explained while the doctor took Eva's temperature and pulse. "He wanted to send you to the hospital in Trutnov, but Frau Hawlik insisted that you'd be safer here. The streets were blocked by snow, so she ordered the guards to bring you back to the camp on a sled."

"You've been lucky," the doctor said as she removed some of the bandages around Eva's head a minute later. "The storm closed the roads from Gros Rosen for two days, so the SS inspectors have been unable to reach us. But we can't take any chances," she added. "Frau Hawlik ordered that you go back to the barracks as soon as it's safe to move you."

Eva was too tired and confused to take in most of what Dr. Sokolow and Rachel were saying. She wept from the pain as the doctor put some ointment on her scalp and wrapped a new bandage around her head and chin, leaving her face exposed. Then Dr. Sokolow handed Eva a small mirror.

Eva blinked at her reflection in horror. The bandage was wrapped like a turban and made her head seem enormous. Her face was swollen and bruised, with dark purple patches around each eye.

"The bruises will go away," Dr. Sokolow reassured her. "Your hair will grow back, too; it's only a matter of time."

Guards lifted Eva on a stretcher and carried her to the barracks, where she was immediately surrounded by friends bringing comfort and scraps of bread. Rosie lent her a pair of thick socks to wear while she was recovering in bed. Dora had kept an aspirin with her for two years, wrapped in a tiny flannel pouch; now she offered it to Eva. But Eva, though touched, refused the medicine, fearing that there might come a time when someone needed it more.

Eva slept for most of the day. In the brief periods when she awoke Rachel fed her cold soup, one teaspoon at a time, and bread that had been softened in chicory coffee.

Late in the afternoon, while Rachel was helping Eva drink some water, several guards burst into the room.

"*Los! Los!*" they shouted. "Get going! Inspection! Line up immediately!"

"Dear God," Rachel murmured with wide, frightened eyes. All around them girls raced to get ready.

"Go — line up," Eva told Rachel faintly. Girls quickly dragged tables and benches across the concrete floor to make room for the inspection.

"We'll go together." Rachel's voice was strong now, determined. She struggled to pull Eva into a sitting position, but

Eva was unable to hold her head up, and it drooped over to one side.

"Line up," Eva said again, gasping in pain as Rachel gently set her back on the mattress.

"I'm not going to leave you," Rachel insisted, and Eva was too exhausted to argue. Rachel's hands felt warm and steady around her own. Tears started in Eva's eyes as she looked up at her sister.

"Achtung!" shouted a guard. The line of girls in the center aisle froze in silence.

A moment later more guards entered, followed by Frau Hawlik and an SS officer in a long black coat and black gloves.

The officer started down the line of prisoners beside Frau Hawlik. Every few moments he stopped to take a longer look at a prisoner before he passed on. Frau Hawlik watched without comment.

At first it seemed that the officer was going to pass Eva's bunk without noticing her or Rachel; then he turned suddenly, pushed a prisoner aside, and leaned over, looking directly at Eva. Rachel stood straight and tall beside her, holding Eva's hand tightly.

"What about this one?" the officer demanded. The skull and crossbones on his cap danced dizzily before Eva's eyes.

"This one is on special assignment," Frau Hawlik told him quietly. "Leave her to me."

"Assignment?" the officer replied with the shadow of a smile. "She can't even stand up." He raised a gloved hand and signaled to a guard.

"Leave her to me!" Frau Hawlik's voice was low and threatening. The officer's smile vanished; he paused for a moment, then lowered his hand and moved on without a word.

"God is watching over us," Rachel whispered a few minutes later when the inspection had ended and the guards and officers had gone. She took a damp cloth and carefully wiped Eva's face wherever it wasn't covered by the bandage. Rachel's voice soothed Eva as much as the touch of the cool cloth on her bruised skin. Rachel was gentle yet strong; like a psalm, Eva thought.

Eva reached up and wrapped her hand around her sister's, grateful that Rachel was beside her.

"God wouldn't have helped us for so long only to abandon us in the end," Rachel said, and Eva believed it. She could believe almost anything, carried along by the unexpected feelings of relief and comfort that enveloped her.

Rachel tucked Eva's blanket around her and kissed her gently. "Sleep now, Eva. Morning will come soon."

S I X T E E N

"SCHNELL, SCHNELL!"

Eva was awakened by men's voices shouting in the yard below the barracks window.

"Faster, you filthy swine!" they screamed. Dogs barked loudly.

An SS inspection? Eva thought anxiously as she sat up and drew her scarf over her head, covering the downy fuzz that was growing in where her hair had been pulled out two months ago. She ran to the nearest window, where dozens of girls were already crowding to see out. It was Sunday and hours before dawn, but the yard below was crowded with people — old people, to judge by their white hair and bald heads, many of which were uncovered.

All the yard lights were off, in accordance with the blackout laws, but a full moon shone brightly in a clear sky, slowly revealing details. At first it was hard to tell if the people were men or women, as they were half-hidden under layers of ragged blankets, which appeared to be their only protection from the winter night. Here and there someone lay on the snow-covered ground, either dead or asleep; still others crawled about on hands and knees. Most had bare hands.

German soldiers with dogs walked through the crowd shouting, *"Aufstehen! Los!* Stand up! Hurry!"* They used their clubs to beat anyone who was lying down, while the dogs barked and strained at the ends of their leashes. Whenever the dogs were quiet for a minute the sound of groaning and wailing came up from the yard, clear and anguished. Occasionally someone's voice carried above the din, crying out in Yiddish or Polish: begging for food or clothes, calling a name.

"They won't survive long in this cold," cried Dora, horrified. "Why don't the guards let them inside?"

"Oh, my God! My sister Natalia!" a woman screamed suddenly at the next window. She turned with a wild look in her eyes and ran from the room, throwing a large red shawl over her shoulders as she ran, and calling, "Talia, Talia!"

Soon everyone in the barracks was crowding in front of a window, looking for a familiar face. Eventually it became clear that the people in the yard were all women or girls. Most of them stood in the dark shadows of the buildings, where it was impossible to see their features. Eva and Rachel hurried to the first floor to try to get a better view, but every window was packed with women and girls from all three floors of the barracks.

What Eva saw, when she finally got close enough to look, stopped her heart as suddenly as if the barracks wall had collapsed and buried her in bricks. An arm's length from the window, and looking back at her, was a woman with white hair half-covered by a filthy rag around her head. Her eyes, too large for her wasted face, seemed to burn in their sockets. Her bony legs were bare and covered with sores. She might have been a hundred years old, or she might have been younger than Eva; it was impossible to tell.

Behind her stood others, their eyes huge in the dark, their faces twisted in expressions of agony and longing, or flat, empty-eyed, as if they were already dead.

"Back to your bunks! Don't leave your bunks!" shouted Bella, scattering the prisoners as she walked through the barracks. Eva and Rachel hurried back upstairs and waited on their bunks for several hours, listening helplessly to the groaning and cries outside, until at last a guard came to let them out for rations. By then the women who had arrived in the night had been moved from the yard to the *Appellplatz,* but they could still be seen, huddled miserably, gray mounds on the snow.

"Please, my sister is there. I have to talk to her!" the woman in the red shawl begged the guard.

"There will be no contact with the prisoners in the *Appellplatz!*" announced the guard sternly. "No talking — no contact at all!"

"Please, if you could give her this sweater —" the woman in the red shawl pleaded, holding out a woolen garment; but the guard repeated his warning.

"They'll freeze to death!" Rachel whispered a minute later as they waited in line for rations. Eva nodded grimly, shivering as she pulled her scarf tighter around her head. Word spread through the line that the women in the *Appellplatz* had been marching for weeks and were going from Germany to another camp somewhere in the East.

"Maybe they'll be put into one of the buildings here," Dora said. "Or they're waiting for trucks." Eva lowered her head silently; she doubted that the emaciated, half-frozen women would get help of any kind.

All at once a shot rang out, and dogs began to bark. Guards

came into the yard from the *Appellplatz*, dragging a dead woman. The body left streaks of blood on the snow.

A minute later more guards came, half-dragging, half-carrying the woman in the red shawl. She struggled in their grasp, shrieking, "Kill me, kill me, too!"

Eva and Rachel left the ration line at once and carried their empty bowls back to their bunks without a word. Eva tried to eat a few bites of bread from their lockers, but it tasted like ashes, and she couldn't swallow it.

"They're going to kill them; they're going to kill us all!" Rachel burst out. "What if the Nazis make Papa march from Bedzin? Or Uncle Nuchem, Auntie, and little David?"

"Maybe they already did," Eva whispered, unable to keep her secret any longer; and tears and words came spilling out, until she told Rachel everything she had heard from Katerina, a year ago.

Rachel hugged Eva close and wept. "I've been having dreams about Bedzin," Rachel said very softly. "I wake up with the feeling that something terrible has happened to Papa."

"What I heard was only another rumor," Eva said desperately.

They held on to each other with all the strength in their arms. From the *Appellplatz* came the sound of women's voices, wailing, calling out in misery.

"Why didn't you tell me sooner?" Rachel wanted to know.

"I was afraid to, afraid it might make you sicker."

"Poor Eva, I've been more of a burden than a help to you."

133

"No, don't say that, Rachel. I don't know what I'd do without you, how I'd go on."

"If anything happened to you, I wouldn't want to live. . . ." Rachel's voice trailed off into tears, and for a while neither of them spoke.

"I want you to promise me something," Rachel said. "If we live through this, when we go home again, you won't try to protect me all the time. You'll let me do my share in everything. You'll let me take care of you, too."

"But I do; I do let you — when my hair was pulled out, you took care of me for days."

"Promise me, Eva."

"I promise."

Rachel put her head on Eva's shoulder. "When we're grown and married, we'll live on the same street —"

"Zawale street, near Papa."

"Near Papa," Rachel agreed.

All that day, and well into the long night, they lay awake on their bunks, listening to the voices crying out from the *Appellplatz,* and after the voices had faded, listening to the silence.

The next morning the *Appellplatz* was empty. The women and girls who had stayed there had been marched from the camp in the night. Fresh snow had fallen, covering their footprints, and hiding the streaks of blood in the yard.

SEVENTEEN

IN THE MIDDLE of March, the Haase textile factory closed down for good, and from then on, the Jewish workers were confined to the camp in Parschnitz.

"Dead soldiers don't need new uniforms," Herr Schmidt explained to the Jewish girls on their last day at the factory, "and a dead government can't pay for them." From all accounts, he said, the Nazi army had run out of everything — fuel, money, weapons, and men to use them. "Even a madman like Hitler can't hold out much longer," he told Eva privately. He predicted that the Soviet army would arrive "any day now" to liberate them.

In Parschnitz the guards locked the prisoners in their barracks, and only allowed them outside twice a day to get food and use the latrines. Rations were cut back to a bowl of cold, milky water in which potatoes had been boiled for the guards. Sometimes a lucky prisoner might get a potato peel or two, but there were no other vegetables in the broth and, worst of all, no bread to go with it. The prisoners, already thin, began to lose weight rapidly.

"They must have a plan for us," Dora told her friends in the first days after the factory closed. "We're young and able, and we're trained workers; maybe they'll send us to work at another factory." Eva tried to convince herself that this was possible, even though Herr Schmidt had reported that most of the other factories in the region had also closed down, many of them months ago.

"At least we're still in the camp," Rachel would say as they sat on their bunks during the short, bleak March days, too hungry and weak to do much but talk or nap. "We still have water and beds and shelter." They wore all of their clothes, wrapping blankets on top of their coats, as the radiators were no longer turned on at all.

"We don't have to walk to Trutnov anymore," Rosie added tiredly.

"Yes, it could be worse," Eva agreed. "It's better to be indoors, anyway, in this weather." Eva couldn't free herself from the memory of the women who had passed through Parschnitz a month ago, and who had seemed to be marching to their deaths. As long as she and Rachel had a roof over their heads, Eva told herself, and the Russians didn't take too much longer, maybe they could make it.

"The SS haven't come to inspect us since the factory closed," Rosie pointed out toward the end of March. "That's a good sign, don't you think?"

"A very good sign," Dora agreed readily. "They must be planning to trade us for German prisoners of war when the Russians get here."

Over and over Dora told them the story of her father, who had been a solider in the Polish army during the Great War, and had been released in a prisoner exchange at the end. If the Germans were planning to trade prisoners, Dora argued, then they'd have to keep the Jewish girls alive.

But as March ended and the first days of April crept by without any change in the rations, Eva began to fear that the Germans had a plan of another kind: to let the prisoners die slowly by starving — or more quickly, from disease.

With their bodies severely weakened, many girls succumbed to typhus, dysentery, and influenza. Early in April, the Germans stopped emptying the latrines in the yard, allowing them to overflow and hastening the spread of illness. The barracks floor became littered with waste, as many of the sick girls were unable to wait to use the latrines. Still others were too weak to climb down from their bunks, and soiled the mattresses where they lay.

Then, one day in April, as the prisoners lined up for morning rations, a miracle occurred: a note was thrown over the brick wall into the camp yard. It was picked up at once by Genia and Tzipora Gelfer, the rabbi's daughters who had worked in the spinning room. The message had been sent by Herr Schmidt, who seemed to know exactly when and where to throw it to avoid being seen by a guard. Genia and Tzipora had been expecting to hear from him, they explained as the note was passed quickly down the line; they had waited at a certain spot by the camp wall every day since the factory closed down. Herr Schmidt's note held a message of hope: Soviet troops were closing in on Trutnov; their numbers were much greater than those of the German army, and a rapid victory was expected. He ended with the words, "God hasn't forgotten you; do not give up!"

After that first note, messages from Herr Schmidt arrived in the yard every few days: Soviet troops were twenty-five kilometers away, then fifteen. German soldiers were fleeing or surrendering without a fight. Only a few days, a week at the most, he promised; then the Russians would be at the camp. The girls read the notes as eagerly as if they had been dropped from heaven by an angel, passing the wrinkled scraps of paper from hand to hand until the penciled words could no longer be read.

Meanwhile Eva and Rachel fought disease the only ways they could: by washing in cold water at the hall sinks, and checking each other's hair for lice, which carried typhus. The rest of the time they spent on their bunks, lying there for hours without moving. They seldom saw their friends except in passing on the stairs or in the food line. News was hastily exchanged: those who had fallen sick; those who had died. Other than Herr Schmidt's notes, no news reached the prisoners from the outside world.

"If the Russians are as close as Herr Schmidt says, then why aren't they here yet?" Rachel asked Eva one morning late in April. She lay on her back on the bunk; in her hand was the latest note from Herr Schmidt, which the rabbi's daughters had retrieved the day before. Its message was brief: "10 km. 2–3 days. Keep up hope."

"Do you remember how the ground shook from the fighting in Sosnowiec, before the Germans marched into Bedzin?" Rachel stopped for a minute, coughing, then went on in a weaker voice. "If they're only ten kilometers away, why don't we see airplanes? Or hear guns?"

"If only I knew." Eva rose to look out the window nearby. She had been asking herself the same questions. "Maybe they went somewhere else," she guessed. "Maybe they're waiting for supplies from Russia." She was too hungry to think. Where were the guards? It was long past the time for morning rations.

"Eva, I heard some girls talking earlier. One of them heard a guard say they were going to poison the water or ship us to Auschwitz."

Eva remained leaning against the windowsill, without moving, without talking. The sun sat above the hills, which were starting to turn green.

"If they were going to kill us, they wouldn't bother feeding us, would they?" Rachel pleaded.

"Yes, I guess — who knows?" She ought to say something to comfort Rachel, Eva sensed vaguely. After a minute she couldn't recall what it was Rachel had asked her, except that it had something to do with food.

"The guards are late again," Eva said. Food. The one thing she could remember, every minute.

"It doesn't make sense," Rachel repeated in the same pleading voice as before.

Eva couldn't tell if her sister was talking about the guards or the Russians, and was about to ask when Dora hurried over, calling for Eva.

"Rosie's sick," she told Rachel and Eva frantically. "Hurry!"

Rachel got up, and they followed Dora to where Rosie lay on her bunk. Her body was burning with fever, and her clothes were soaked with sweat, while the mattress and blanket were soiled with her waste. Her eyes were open, but she seemed to be in a trance and didn't respond when Dora spoke to her.

Rachel started to cry, while Eva watched Rosie in silent anguish, trying to make out a glimmer of consciousness in her friend's unseeing eyes. If it weren't for Rosie's shallow, labored breathing and an occasional spasm in her legs, she might have been dead.

"She's been feverish for two days, and complaining of cramps in her stomach, but it didn't seem serious — until yesterday," Dora said, her face ashen and drawn.

Rachel began to cough, holding her kerchief over her mouth.

"Last night she kept begging for water," Dora went on desperately. "At first I tried giving her a bit of soup I had saved, but she couldn't keep anything down, even water. Then I must have fallen asleep, and when I woke up —" Dora took one of Rosie's limp hands in her own and rubbed it gently. "As soon as the guards open the doors we have to get her to the infirmary," she said with sudden energy. "Dr. Sokolow will make her well."

"The infirmary is full," Eva tried to warn Dora. "Besides, Dr. Sokolow says that there's nothing she can do for dysentery."

"Who says it's dysentery? There was something bad in the soup, that's all."

Eva put her arm around Dora without a word. Just then, Rachel's coughing grew worse, rattling in her chest as if something were shaking loose inside her. Eva helped Rachel back to bed and stayed with her until the attack had passed and she was resting quietly.

Finally, the guards opened the doors for morning rations. Dora found two more girls to help her and Eva, and together they wrapped Rosie in a clean blanket and lifted her from the bunk. Rosie had lost so much weight that it wasn't hard for them to carry her. After some pleading from Dora, Dr. Sokolow agreed to take Rosie in the infirmary. But from the look on Dr. Sokolow's face Eva knew there wasn't much hope.

Eva left the infirmary and went out to join Rachel, who was waiting for her in the food line. Her mouth began to water as she crossed the yard, and her only thought, while she looked for Rachel in the line, was whether there'd be some peels in their broth.

Just then Frau Hawlik walked toward the prisoners with a guard.

"I need thirty strong workers to dig ditches!" the guard shouted. "Hot stew and bread for anyone who works!" Girls left the line at once to crowd around the guard, pushing one another to get closer, but the guard turned most of them away immediately. "You're not strong enough," she told one prisoner after another. "I need people who can work hard."

Eva hesitated for a moment, straightening her clothes and kerchief, then forced her way into the jostling crowd.

"Let me see your hair, Bedzin," Frau Hawlik called out jovially when she caught sight of Eva. "Why don't you take off your kerchief for once?"

Eva's face burned as she drew back her kerchief, revealing the cap of downy fuzz that covered the top of her head. Below it, around the sides and back, her graying hair fell in thin, tangled strands.

"A chicken! A plucked chicken!" Frau Hawlik laughed, enjoying her joke. "You were lucky, Bedzin," she told Eva, still chuckling. "Last year a girl died after her braid was pulled out by one of those machines."

At first Eva couldn't speak; then she summoned the remaining shreds of her courage and raised her head to face the *Lagerführerin*.

"I want to dig ditches," Eva told her.

Frau Hawlik did not appear to have heard, and busied herself with locating a cube of sugar in one of the pockets of her long black coat. After she had found the sugar and put it on her tongue, she let her gaze, coolly appraising, focus once more on Eva.

"This one is strong enough," Frau Hawlik informed the guard, who wrote Eva's number in a notebook and told her to report to the front gate in half an hour.

Rachel was terrified when she heard the news. "What if it's a trick?" she whispered while she and Eva ate their soup in the barracks a few minutes later. "What if they take you to Auschwitz?" She held Eva's arm. "Don't go, Eva," she pleaded. "Just hide somewhere until the guard's gone."

"I have to go, Rachel; the guard wrote down my number. Besides, think of the bread and stew!" Eva bent to wrap pieces of twine around her shoes, which were coming apart so badly that she had to hold them together with string. She fumbled with the knots as she tied them.

"You're nothing but skin and bones," Rachel went on. "How are you going to dig ditches? What will the guards do to you if you can't?" She began to cry. "Don't go, Eva! Don't let us be separated. With Rosie sick —" She stopped suddenly, coughing into her kerchief, fighting for breath. Finally, exhausted, she finished hoarsely, "I can face anything as long as you're with me."

Eva hesitated as she considered Rachel's words, but her gnawing hunger and the sound of Rachel's coughing were stronger than any other arguments. Rachel finished her soup and lay down at once; the effort of talking had used up the last of her strength. Eva studied Rachel's feverish face and knew she would probably not leave her bed again that day.

"Stay warm, and try to sleep," Eva whispered as she spread Rachel's blanket, then her own, over her sister's shivering body. "I'll be back with stew and bread for supper," she added, then took her coat and her bowl and went outside to the gate.

E I G H T E E N

THE GERMAN ARMY truck clattered along the stone-paved streets of Parschnitz and Trutnov, then into open countryside, where unplowed farm fields lay covered with ice-crusted puddles. Crowded with Eva in the open truck were thirty girls from the camp and three armed soldiers. It was the first time Eva had been out of the camp since the factory had closed six weeks earlier.

Although it was April and a clear day, the air still held winter's sting. Buds were just beginning to open on shrubs along the roadside, and patches of old, gray snow lingered under trees and on the high meadows of the foothills. The morning mist rose like a curtain being lifted, and despite her hunger, Eva drank in the sights that were revealed — red and blue shirts on a line; an old horse, lifting his head to stare at the truck — as eagerly as if she were sitting in a dark theater, waiting for a play to begin. Memories crowded into her thoughts: muddy April roads in the countryside near Bedzin, where she went for long walks with her family; picnic lunches in the shade of old stone hay sheds.

At a crossroads the truck turned onto an unpaved road where

potholes and soft mud forced it to slow down. They hadn't gone far before they began to meet a steady stream of travelers on wagons, horses, bikes, and on foot.

All of them were going the same direction — away from wherever the truck was heading; and all the travelers were ragged and covered with dirt, as if they had been on the road for many days.

"Give us a lift!" they called in German to the soldiers on the truck. Fear and desperation were written in their eyes. "We're German citizens, loyal Germans," they pleaded, but the soldiers only waved them away impatiently.

"*Abhauen!* Out of the way!" the soldiers shouted over and over, and the driver blared his horn; even so, the truck was forced to stop and wait, again and again, for wagons that had gotten stuck in the mud.

Once, a soldier had to jump down to help move a cart piled high with belongings which was being pulled by two young girls and an old woman. Eva overheard them talking, asking the soldier questions: how far away the Russians were, whether it was safe to stop in Trutnov for the night, whether it was true that Hitler had surrendered.

Eva's spirits rose at the sight of these German people running from the Soviet army. Here at last was proof that the Russians were close. This, combined with the promise of stew and bread, gave Eva the first real hope she had felt in weeks.

At one point the truck passed an old woman struggling to carry a wooden cage in which a live chicken roosted. "Better leave the chicken with me!" one of the soldiers called down to her. He laughed as he reached for the cage.

"You'll have to kill me first!" shouted the old woman furiously, jumping back with surprising energy. "I'd rather give it to the Russians!"

"Then you're going the wrong way, old woman!" called the soldier as the truck passed. The other soldiers didn't seem to share his high spirits, and looked somber at the reference to Russians.

After they had traveled for about an hour Eva heard the first sounds of gunfire in the distance. Soon they began to pass German army vehicles parked along the side of the road, and small groups of soldiers carrying shovels and pickaxes. The truck bumped across a train track, then stopped beside a small rural train platform, where the prisoners were ordered out.

They were given shovels and led into a field covered with stubble from last year's crops. A dozen soldiers were already at work, digging in a waist-deep trench running partway across the field; a row of stakes marked where the trench was to be extended. Every shovelful of earth cast up by the soldiers added to a ridge of mud running along the top of the trench. Many of the soldiers were older than her father, Eva noticed with surprise as she crossed the field. Some of them appeared to be as ill-suited for their work as the emaciated Jewish girls: one soldier had lost a hand; another was on crutches.

So this is the mighty German army, Eva thought, gathering courage at every new sign of German weakness. She felt no fear when a blast of gunfire shook the ground a moment later; she almost welcomed it, as a signal of her approaching liberation.

But as soon as she began to work, Eva forgot everything except her hunger and the pain in her hands, arms, and shoulders. Her muscles cried out every time that she pried a shovelful of rocks and mud from the sodden ground, then hauled it up to the top of the trench. The deeper the trench grew, the higher she had to throw the mud. As the hours passed, her hands became red and swollen, then blisters began to form on her fingers and palms. Eventually the blisters cracked, exposing tender new skin.

Eva worked on numbly. Sometimes an image of stew and bread came into her thoughts, driving her on; more often she couldn't think at all. Once, the girl beside her lost her grip on the shovel, splattering dirt and pebbles on top of Eva's head where the skin was still healing. Eva started to cry out from the pain, but stopped herself when she saw a soldier walking only meters away. All through the morning, while the sun rose higher in the pale sky, Eva lifted shovelfuls of mud as if in a nightmare. It seemed like days had passed when a soldier finally called for them to stop work. Eva loosened her stiff fingers from the shovel and crawled painfully out of the trench.

A soldier was dishing out stew from large iron kettles on the back of a truck. The strong, savory smell followed Eva as she washed the dirt from her hands in a nearby stream, then hurried to line up with the other prisoners. Her fingers hurt so badly that she could barely hold her bowl and spoon.

"There's pork in the stew," a woman told Eva when she joined the line.

"How do you know?" Eva asked, horrified. The Torah forbade eating pork or anything that had come into contact with it.

"I heard the soldiers talking," the woman replied.

"It's pork, all right," said another woman, whose dirty red hair bristled like pieces of straw around the edges of her blue kerchief. "I saw it with my own eyes."

"What would you know about pork?" asked another girl, shocked.

The woman with red hair shrugged. "I know, that's all."

"I'm sure the rabbis would say it's all right to eat pork in our case," decided a woman whose hands were shaking so badly that the spoon rattled in her bowl.

"God forgive me," said someone else, praying in Hebrew as she moved forward in the line.

"Are you going to eat yours?" the woman with red hair asked Eva.

Eva shook her head, blinking back tears of frustration. The smell of the food nearly drove her wild, but she couldn't eat pork, couldn't break God's commandment just to satisfy her hunger. Not even now.

"Why don't we trade — your stew for my bread," the woman suggested. Eva agreed readily; at least she'd still have something to eat, and to take back to Rachel. She felt better yet when she left the food line a few minutes later with two small loaves of black bread, still warm from baking. But just as Eva sat down to eat, a soldier limped over and ordered Eva and two other girls to unload some bags of sand.

"I'll watch your bread," offered the red-haired woman at once.

"*Vorwärts!* Let's go!" the soldier said impatiently as Eva hesitated. She handed over the loaves with reluctance and hurried after the limping soldier.

He led Eva and the two other girls to the far end of the train platform, where he ordered them to unload bags of sand from trucks, then stack the bags on the platform. The girls worked in a line, passing the heavy sand from person to person; but Eva's hands hurt so badly that she dropped half of the bags. After watching for a minute the soldier pulled Eva from the line and replaced her with another girl. Quickly examining Eva's hands, he took out a first-aid kit from one of the trucks and applied a thick ointment to her fingers and palms, then wrapped them in clean bandages. For a minute Eva's hands stung as if pins were sticking into them, then the stinging subsided and with it, some of the throbbing pain.

"Better?" the soldier asked.

"Much better, thank you," Eva told him, surprised to be treated with consideration. Perhaps the soldier didn't know that she was Jewish; or, more puzzling still, perhaps it didn't matter to him.

The soldier dismissed Eva, and she went back at once to claim her food, but the red-haired woman looked sorry to see her, then told Eva that her loaves had been stolen.

"That cheating Hungarian took them, she and her friend!" the red-haired woman cried, pointing at two women who crouched on the dirt, scraping the last stew from their bowls. They looked up in surprise.

"That's a lie!" one of them replied, rising with furious energy. "She ate both loaves herself, the Polish maggot!" The two women began to scream at each other in several languages at once.

Eva walked away, shaking with hunger and rage, then sat down by the stream to try to fill her empty stomach with water. The German soldier had been kinder than these Jewish women, she reflected bitterly. Tears of frustration ran down her cheeks, where the rough-handed wind dried them. Still, it was her own fault she'd lost the bread; she should have known better than to trust her food to anyone. As she bent to drink from the stream, she tried to comfort herself with the thought that there'd be another meal that evening.

But there was no other meal, although the girls worked until long after dark. Some of them collapsed from pain or exhaustion, and lay for hours in the muddy trench, where the soldiers ignored them. The evening was very cold and very quiet, except for sporadic explosions of artillery. By the time the soldiers told them to quit, Eva was barely able to stand up and could no longer lift her shovel. The girls who could still walk helped those who couldn't back to the truck, where they all huddled together for warmth on the trip back to Parschnitz. Eva almost rejoiced when they arrived at the camp.

Rachel was waiting for her just inside the barracks. "I was afraid you wouldn't come back again," Rachel said, crying in anguish as she threw her arms around Eva.

"I was cheated of my food," Eva said, resting her head on her sister's shoulder. "I have nothing to give you."

Rachel didn't seem to hear her. "Rosie's gone," she said, sobbing and clinging to Eva. She began to cough, and covered her mouth with her kerchief; after a minute she caught her breath and went on.

"Guards came and took Rosie — they took anyone who was too sick to stand up. Dora wasn't there; she'd been called out to clean the guards' barracks." Rachel's words came out in short bursts, broken by crying and coughing; and Eva, numb with exhaustion and shock, only half-understood what she heard.

"Dora blames herself," Rachel added. "She says — if she had taken better care of her, Rosie wouldn't have died."

Died. The word cut like a knife through Eva's confused thoughts.

"The guards didn't even try to hide where they were taking the sick girls —"

"No, don't say it," Eva begged.

They climbed the stairs slowly, leaning on each other and the rail. The moment they reached the third floor, Eva went over to Dora's bunk, where Dora lay awake with one of Rosie's shirts in her arms, clinging to it as if it were human. Eva lay down beside her and put her arms around both Dora and the shirt. Neither of them said anything, and neither cried.

The muffled booming of artillery could be heard now, very faint in the distance. If the Russians had come sooner, Eva thought, Rosie could have lived to become an opera singer in Palestine. Eva stayed until Dora fell asleep, then dragged herself back to her bunk.

"I saved some soup for you," Rachel said when Eva returned. The bowl that Rachel offered her was almost full.

"Didn't you eat?"

"I wasn't hungry."

Eva insisted that Rachel drink half of the cold broth, then quickly drained what was left and lay down on her bunk.

"The Russians are very close, Rachel," Eva whispered. "Listen, you can hear their guns."

Rachel nodded silently as she removed Eva's bandage, which was filthy and bloodstained, then began to wash Eva's hands with a wet cloth.

"I have to go back; we didn't finish the trench," Eva told her, gasping when the cloth touched her raw skin.

"Go back! How can you hold a shovel?"

Eva was quiet for a minute. "It's not so bad," she said at last. "Tomorrow I'll be smarter. I'll bring back some food."

"Tomorrow I'll go with you."

That was impossible, Eva knew; even if the guards allowed her to go, Rachel could never handle the work. But Eva was too tired to argue about it, even to think about it. She fell asleep as soon as Rachel finished cleaning her hands.

Early in the morning Eva was awakened by something hitting her in the ribs. "*Los!* Get going!" a guard snapped, prodding her with a club. "At the gate in ten minutes!" The guard moved on through the room, waking other girls.

Every muscle in Eva's body protested as she made herself stand up. Rachel got up at the same moment and started to put on her shoes, but she was coughing badly and had to stop frequently to catch her breath.

"It's too much for you," Eva protested feebly as she went downstairs a few minutes later, with Rachel at her side. Still, Eva was secretly relieved to have Rachel with her.

"I won't let you leave me again," Rachel said with an arm around Eva, and Eva answered her with a grateful hug.

But they hadn't gone halfway across the yard when a guard stopped them, forced them apart with his club, and ordered Rachel back to the barracks.

N I N E T E E N

SHARP BURSTS OF gunfire exploded in the distance. *The Soviet army* must *have reached the trench by now,* Eva thought, as she listened from her bunk. How many days had passed since she had gone to dig the trench? It was May, she knew, but she couldn't recall which day it was, or how many days she'd fallen asleep and awakened again to the sound of artillery. Events were starting to blur in her memory.

What could be keeping the Russians? After she had seen the condition of the German soldiers and had watched the German civilians running away, Eva had expected the Soviet army to arrive quickly. But, still, the distant guns boomed, without getting closer and without end. Still, the girls waited, starving and sick.

"Maybe there will be bread today," Dora said, stopping by Eva's bunk on her way to line up for morning rations.

Eva almost smiled at this. Bread! Only Dora could imagine such a possibility. But hunger commanded Eva to get up, and besides, she needed to use the latrine — if there was still a latrine that had not overflowed. She pulled herself up with an effort.

On the bunk beside her, Rachel was still sleeping; she slept most of the time now. The skin on her arms and face was covered with beads of sweat, and there were pink patches on her neck and cheeks. It was the heat in the barracks, Eva told herself as she reached over to wipe the sweat from Rachel's face. The minute the weather had turned warm outside, it became stifling in the old brick building where hundreds of women were packed in without any fresh air.

Eva took Rachel's bowl and her own, then started shakily after Dora. Neither of them could move quickly on their bony legs; and Dora's feet were swollen from an infection, so that just standing brought tears to her eyes. Nearly everyone in the camp was sick with something, but the infirmary had been closed for over a week, and the doctors were gone. Guards came into the barracks twice a day to carry out the dead. Sometimes the guards made mistakes; it wasn't always easy to tell who was dead and who was sleeping.

When Eva and Dora reached the front door they found a small crowd of women and girls waiting for the guards. One girl banged her metal bowl on the door. "Let us out!" she called in a shrill, rasping voice. "Give us our rations."

"Are you crazy, shouting at the guards? They'll kill us all!" cried one of the others, trying to stop her.

"Listen to her!" said the first girl sarcastically. "She's made a great discovery: the Germans are going to kill us!"

"The water has been turned off," announced someone who had just joined them. "I tried faucets on every floor."

"Five years," whispered a young woman, stroking her bald head with a trembling hand. "I came through; I stayed alive. For what? So these Nazi butchers could starve me." She fell silent, her eyes veiled by grief.

"Master of creation," one of the women prayed quietly, "may the Russians come today."

"Amen," mumbled many voices at once.

Eva slid through the crowd and looked out the window. The yard appeared to be deserted. An eerie silence hung over the camp; other than the distant explosions, there was no sound at all.

Where were the guards? Had they abandoned the camp and left the prisoners to die? Eva felt no fear at the thought of dying, only great sadness. All she wanted was to go back upstairs to Rachel, to sleep; not to face whatever might happen. She leaned wearily against the door, trying to will enough strength into her legs to walk up the stairs.

Just then the roar of an engine shattered the silence, and someone sped past the window on a motorcycle. The rider wore men's pants and a leather jacket; a bit of yellow hair showed beneath a leather helmet. A guard appeared from a building, ran to open the gate, and saluted as the rider tore through.

"It's Frau Hawlik!" cried one of the girls beside Eva. "Frau Hawlik's leaving!"

"She's right! I saw her face!" Everyone pressed close to the window and began to talk at once. They all agreed that the *Lagerführerin*'s sudden departure could only mean one thing: the Russians must be closing in on Parschnitz. The girls and women hugged one another, and their voices grew animated with restored hope.

"God will answer our prayers now," one girl said.

"You think God cares what happens to us?" muttered another. "God left long ago, even before Frau Hawlik!"

"The Russians will be here today! We'll have real food for dinner!" Dora said as she and Eva dragged themselves upstairs to share the news.

"But why are the guards still here?" Eva worried, leaning on the handrail to catch her breath. "What if Frau Hawlik comes back?"

"Who knows? Maybe she ordered the guards to stay, to carry out the prisoner exchange." As for the chance of Frau Hawlik returning, Dora refused to take the idea seriously. The fact that the *Lagerführerin* had disguised herself as a civilian, and a man, was proof that she was trying to escape.

By the time Eva reached the third floor, those who were well enough to get up had already gathered at the window in a state of anxious anticipation. Rachel woke up and asked Eva for water. She was shivering and short of breath, and complained that her head was buzzing. She tried to sit up but she couldn't support her head, and lay down again almost immediately.

"There's no water right now, Rachel, but I think there will be, soon," Eva said, and tried to tell her sister about Frau Hawlik's departure.

But Rachel wouldn't listen, and pushed Eva's hand away fretfully. "You just want it all for yourself. Why are you being so mean? Can't you see how thirsty I am?" she complained in a wheezy voice, coughing frequently while she spoke. She didn't raise her hand to cover her mouth.

"The Russians are coming; just a little longer, Rachel," Eva went on patiently, reaching over with Rachel's kerchief to wipe some drops of phlegm from her sister's mouth.

"Why won't you help me?" Rachel whimpered; then her eyes closed, and she became so quiet that Eva thought she was asleep. A minute later Rachel began complaining again: "My head is pounding, Eva; make it stop."

"I'm sorry, Rachel. Try to wait, just a little longer," Eva whispered. "The moment the Russians get here I'll get you some water, I promise."

For the rest of the day Eva stayed beside Rachel, who slept fitfully, waking frequently to ask for water. Dora came over to report on her observations from the window: a guard had crossed the yard; trucks were heard on the street outside the camp. Finally, everyone drifted back to their bunks, too tired to watch at the window any longer. Day faded slowly into night.

In the middle of the night Eva was awakened by screams. Several girls stood at the windows, sobbing hysterically. "They're going to burn us alive!" they cried. Outside, strange glowing clouds swirled high into the air. For a moment Eva thought she was dreaming; then she got up to look. A building across the yard was on fire; smoke and orange flames poured from the roof and illuminated the windows. As Eva pushed her way closer she saw that other buildings were on fire as well. One of them was the building that was rumored to store explosives.

Eva glanced back toward Rachel, who was still asleep. More and more girls crowded by the window, praying, weeping, or watching in stunned silence.

Just then some dark forms appeared in the yard below, moving quickly through the smoky haze and dragging hoses behind them. Guns went off, but the people in the yard kept coming, shouting in Czech as they smashed windows and aimed their hoses into the fire. Shouts and gunshots mingled with the sound of breaking glass and the roar of the blaze. The smoke became so thick that it was like trying to see through a cloud. Dora joined Eva by the window, and the two of them watched, silent and numb, barely able to make out what was happening. Smoke began to creep inside the barracks, and girls held their sleeves in front of their faces, coughing as the fumes grew stronger.

How could Rachel have slept through all the noise? Eva worried. She made her way to Rachel's bunk to reassure herself that her sister was breathing, then returned once more to the window.

It might have been hours or only minutes later when the flames finally died away, leaving a few, smoldering traces. The people who had put out the fire departed as suddenly as they had come; after one final volley of gunfire the camp fell silent. One by one, most of the girls went back to bed, but Dora and Eva remained at the window for a long time, watching to see what might happen. As the smoke began to clear, several bodies became visible among the pieces of charred wood and debris in the yard. A full moon illuminated the scene.

"It's a guard," Eva said as she made out the Nazi emblem on one of the uniforms.

"They're all guards," said Dora, peering out at the dark forms on the ground. "Why hasn't anyone come to take them away?"

They waited a while longer, and still, there was no sign of life in the yard.

"Maybe the other guards ran away," Dora suggested hopefully. "Maybe the Czech people killed them."

"I'm going out to get water," Eva said, taking her bowl from the locker and heading toward the stairs. *One more hour,* she heard Papa's voice as she made her way through the dark room. *Try to stay alive for one more hour.*

"What if it's a trap?" Dora asked. "What if guards are waiting to kill us as we leave?" But she grabbed her bowl and followed Eva down the stairs.

When they reached the first floor, some of the other girls had already broken a window and were climbing out into the yard. Eva and Dora followed them, stepping cautiously onto a pile of boards under the window. Every building in the camp was dark and silent, and appeared to have been abandoned, but Eva couldn't help looking around nervously as they drank from a faucet, then filled their bowls. Other prisoners filed past them through the yard, looking more like skeletons in rags than like women or girls. They headed for the guards' barracks, the kitchen, and the house of Frau Hawlik and Fräulein Kirschlag.

"We'd better get some food before it's all gone," Dora said. "You take the water and I'll bring back whatever I can."

Eva watched Dora heading toward Frau Hawlik's house, then climbed back into the barracks with the water and started slowly upstairs, managing not to spill too much on the way.

Rachel was awake, but distracted and feverish, and didn't seem to understand when Eva told her about the fire and the guards. Eva helped Rachel sit up and supported her while she drank one of the bowls of water. The minute she finished drinking, Rachel fell back on her mattress and was asleep immediately. Eva drank part of the other bowl, then lay down beside her, dizzy and exhausted, and was nearly sleeping when Dora came back a short time later.

"This is all I could get," Dora said, handing Eva a small crust of stale bread before she, too, lay down. By the time she'd reached Frau Hawlik's pantry, everything else had been taken, Dora reported; she'd had to fight two other girls for the bread. All the guards were gone, she said.

"Fräulein Kirschlag was there," Dora went on. "Some girls found her in her room and killed her with their bare hands — strangled her."

Eva listened numbly, barely comprehending. She broke the crust into three shares, then chewed her piece in silence. Beside her, Dora ate her piece and drank the remaining water.

"I'll get more water in the morning," Eva said.

"We can have all we want," Dora agreed.

Eva raised herself to sprinkle the last drops of water onto Rachel's burning cheeks and brow, then lay down again in the hot, smoky room between her sister and her friend, and fell asleep.

T W E N T Y

FOR THREE DAYS after the fire the camp yard remained deserted, empty of life except for those girls, thin as shadows, who stumbled out into the sunshine to fill their metal bowls with water. Some of the prisoners moved into Frau Hawlik's house, where the toilets were soon broken from overuse.

Trucks and wagons passed the camp, but no one came to open the gates. No one brought food. The distant thunder of artillery faded, then disappeared completely. And still the prisoners, fewer each day, waited.

Rachel's fever climbed sharply and she slept day and night, waking up only to cry out from pain in her head or stomach. Her body was convulsed continuously by tremors, as if she were in the hands of an unseen force bent on shaking her to death. Eva made trip after trip to the yard, and spread cool water on Rachel's burning face, neck, and arms, but Rachel's fever did not go down. Each trip to the yard took Eva an hour, as she had to sit down frequently to rest.

"The Russians aren't going to come here at all," Dora said on the morning of the fourth day after the fire. "They've forgotten about us, or they don't care."

Eva sat beside her, picking lice from under the collar of Rachel's dress, then squashing them between her fingernails. All around them girls moaned and cried out in their sleep.

"Rachel's worse," Eva said suddenly. "Her rash has spread."

"How far?"

"I can't tell. Help me get her dress off."

"If we could unlock the gates, we could go out and get food ourselves," Dora said as she helped Eva unbutton Rachel's dress. Rachel was so thin that Eva could nearly circle her waist with both hands.

"Dear God, no!" Eva whispered as she pulled back Rachel's dress, exposing a bright pink rash across her chest.

"Typhus," Dora announced in a grim voice. She pulled a string of lice from the shoulder seam of Rachel's dress. The tiny insects were swollen with Rachel's blood.

Eva began to sob while Dora set about killing the lice methodically.

"I'll wash her hair, her body, her clothes — everything," Eva cried. *Oh, God, no! Don't let her die.*

"I'll help you get the water."

"No, you shouldn't walk." Dora's right foot was covered with open sores; in the last two days it had swollen to several times its usual size.

"Take my shoes, then," Dora offered. "I'll check the rest of Rachel's clothes and get rid of the lice."

Eva put on Dora's shoes and was halfway downstairs with their bowls when she heard shouting in the yard, then heavy pounding at the front door, as if someone was trying to break it down. Eva froze, horrified: was it the Nazis, coming back to kill them?

Then the pounding stopped, and a man shouted, "*Frei — frei!* You are free!" Dazed, Eva started down the stairs again. At the entrance the large wooden doors had been broken off their hinges, then thrown into the yard. Eva squinted into the bright daylight, barely comprehending what she saw: across the yard, only a few meters away, the camp gates were open.

She hobbled toward them slowly, painfully, her shriveled legs nearly buckling with every step. The harsh glare made her head swim. A noisy swarm of wagons, trucks, and people passed on the street. Eva reached the gates and held on to keep herself from falling, then stared at the spectacle before her.

A dead horse lay on the street, its belly swollen to a monstrous size. People on foot or bicycle steered around the animal, swearing and holding handkerchiefs over their noses. Wagons and cars drove partway onto the sidewalk to get past.

This was a dream, Eva told herself; it had to be. Soon she would wake up and the Germans would be there, shouting: "*Mach schnell!* Hurry! Line up!" And the dream would end.

A young man on a motorcycle pulled up beside Eva. He held a Russian flag in one hand. When he saw Eva he jumped off his motorcycle and embraced her, kissing her on both cheeks. His face shone with joy.

"You should be smiling, Grandmother!" he exclaimed.

"Please, can you get us a doctor?" Eva asked him, still holding on to the gate for support. Maybe it wasn't a dream after all. "My sister is sick," she went on. "Please — we need a doctor — also food and hot water."

"There's a hospital in Trutnov," the motorcyclist said uneasily, then he backed off and stared in growing alarm as a stream of emaciated girls emerged from the barracks and shuffled toward him across the yard. They moved as if they were just learning how to walk; some, too weak to stand, were crawling on hands and knees.

"Saints and apostles." The motorcyclist crossed himself. "I will see what I can do," he told Eva in a choked voice, then he swung his leg over his motorcycle and rode off.

After he left, Eva tried to focus her thoughts, which seemed as slow to function as her legs. Food first: for herself, Dora, and Rachel. Then a doctor. There was a bakery down the street, she recalled, and shuffled slowly along the sidewalk in that direction, stumbling on the paving stones and grasping the brick walls for support.

Hold on, Rachel. Please hold on.

She hadn't gone far before she had to stop and rest, leaning wearily against the wall, which held the sun's warmth in its red bricks.

A little boy ran up and reached out to touch her. "Mama, look! A bone lady!"

His mother hurried after him and pulled him back. "Don't

touch her!" she cried sharply, looking at Eva with a mixture of pity and horror.

"She's alive!" the boy persisted, trying to break from his mother's grasp, but she held him firmly by the arm and led him away. Eva thought to ask the woman for food, but she was already halfway across the street.

The bakery had been broken into and looted, Eva found. The shelves were bare, and broken glass lay everywhere. Leaving the noisy main street, Eva turned down a narrow, curving side street and began to knock at doors. Many homes appeared to be deserted; through the front windows Eva saw clothes and quilts scattered on floors, and partly eaten meals left on tables. She would have liked to take some of the food or clothing, but she was afraid to go inside, afraid the owners might come back and find her.

At one house an old woman looked down at Eva from a second-story window and growled, "You Jews are still alive?" then slammed the window closed.

Finally, a girl about her age answered the door at a narrow stone house, and hurried to bring Eva a small brown jug of milk, a half-loaf of bread, and a piece of cheese.

"You are welcome — most welcome," the girl said in a mix of German and Czech when Eva thanked her for the food. She wanted Eva to come into her kitchen, but Eva refused, ashamed of how filthy and ragged she was, and sat on the front step to eat her meal of bread and cheese. The girl watched with tears in her eyes, and Eva nearly wept, too, so wonderful did the food taste.

She had forgotten that bread could be moist and sweet, or that milk was so creamy and refreshing. And the cheese was best of all: mildly nutty, it seemed to grow more delicious with every mouthful.

"Is there a doctor in town?" Eva asked while she ate, but the girl shook her head. There had been a German doctor, she said, but he had left Parschnitz some time ago.

Eva would have liked to savor this glorious food longer, but after only a few bites she began to feel full. Just as well, she reflected; with careful rationing the bread and cheese could feed Dora, Rachel, and herself for two days. Eva forced herself to stand up, and reluctantly handed back the crockery jug, which was more than half full.

"Keep it," the girl urged. "Come again and I'll refill it. My grandfather is going fishing," she added. "Tomorrow I'll bake fish cakes. Please come back; I always make plenty."

Eva thanked the girl again and started back to the camp with the bread, cheese, and milk held tightly in her arms. Her steps were a little steadier now. *Hold on, Rachel; only a little longer.*

But when she turned back onto the main street, she found army trucks parked near the camp, and more trucks driving into the gates. *Oh, God, no!* she thought. *The Germans have come back to kill us!*

Then Eva saw that there was something different about the soldiers who were unloading the trucks and carrying boxes through the gates. Some of them wore shabby, soiled uniforms, but many wore only part of a uniform, or ordinary work clothes. No one had Nazi swastikas or SS skulls on their jackets. The men bantered and laughed as they worked. They were speaking Russian.

One of the soldiers saw Eva and started toward her. "May I help you with your load, little sister?" he said in broken German. He held out his hand to Eva; a long scar ran across the back of his wrist.

Eva stepped back from the soldier and hugged her food closer.

"Please don't be afraid," he said. "We're soldiers of the Soviet army; we've come to help you." The soldier was smiling, but he had sad eyes and a gentle voice. "You are free now," he went on softly. "Germany has surrendered. Hitler is dead."

Hitler dead — and she was free! Eva felt as if her brain would explode. Suddenly she understood: the Germans had not come back; they were never coming back. Her legs buckled under her, and she fell on the pavement, dropping the jug. "Oh, my God; no!" she cried, reaching for it, but it had broken into pieces.

"Don't worry," the soldier said. "There's plenty more —"

"You don't understand," Eva said, and sobbed as the precious milk ran into the street. "This is for my sister —"

"We are preparing a meal for all of you now," the soldier reassured her. "There will be food tonight, tomorrow, and every day."

"My sister is very sick," Eva told him, wiping her tears with a trembling hand. "Do you have a doctor? She needs a doctor right away."

"We are setting up an infirmary as fast as possible. Our doctor, Major Dufkovsky, is expected to arrive this evening."

"Her name is Rachel Buchbinder. Third floor, Barracks One. Please, you must tell the doctor about her as soon as he arrives. And my friend's foot is infected."

"You can show me yourself." The soldier held out his hand to help Eva up.

Eva tried to stand, but her legs would not support her, so the soldier lifted her and carried her through the yard as easily as if she were a baby.

Jeeps, cars, and open trucks crowded into the *Appellplatz*. A huge bonfire had been built, and soldiers ran in and out of the barracks, throwing blankets and mattresses into the flames. To Eva, the healthy young soldiers seemed to have the strength of giants.

As soon as the soldier carried Eva into the barracks he was surrounded by girls begging for food. "Be patient, sisters," he told them. "Tonight you will eat porridge and bread, I promise you."

The Russian soldiers had already restored cold water to the barracks. They had also stripped the vermin-infested blankets and mattresses from the bunks and replaced them with clean blankets.

Rachel lay curled up on a blanket, fighting for air in long, wheezing breaths, and shivering violently. Dora sat beside her, holding her hand.

The soldier covered Rachel with another blanket, then

looked at Dora's foot and made some notes in a small book he carried in his pocket.

"I'll speak to the doctor as soon as he arrives," he promised Eva and Dora, filling their bowls with water before he left.

"I got rid of all the lice," Dora told Eva anxiously. "I wanted to give Rachel my aspirin, but I couldn't find it." She started to cry. "I don't know what happened; I looked everywhere."

"It's all right. The Soviet army doctor will be here soon," Eva said. She gave the bread and cheese to Dora, who began to eat at once.

"Rachel, wake up." Eva reached out to stroke her sister's cheek. "Rachel, dearest — I brought you some food —"

"Papa." Rachel's voice was so soft that Eva wasn't sure if she had heard the word or imagined it. "Papa," Rachel repeated hoarsely, opening her eyes and fixing them on Eva. Rachel's skin was covered with beads of sweat, and her eyes had sunken so far back in her head that it looked like an empty skull.

Dear God, no!

"It's Eva, Rachel." Eva fought against her fear and took one of Rachel's wasted hands in her own.

"I was — waiting —" Rachel managed in a rasping whisper.

"I brought you water and bread — please try to eat —" Eva wiped the sweat from her sister's brow. "The Russians have come, Rachel. They're going to feed us; they'll make you well again." She struggled to raise Rachel's head. "Drink, Rachel."

Rachel's lips were swollen and cracked. Eva held the bowl to her mouth, but Rachel pushed it away, spilling half of the water.

"Just a little," Eva pleaded, but Rachel kept her lips pressed together. Eva gently lowered her sister's head onto the bunk.

"I'm — late," Rachel said between breaths.

"Late? For what? What are you talking about?" Eva whispered in horror.

"School — I didn't bring —"

"What school?" Tears ran down Eva's face. "Rachel, don't talk like this! You're frightening me."

"Stay here," Rachel whimpered pitifully. Her eyelids closed again.

"Drink some water, Rachel," Eva begged. "The Russian doctor will be here soon. You have to hold on." *Dear God, don't take her from me now.*

Rachel showed no sign that she had heard. Her chest rose and fell; each rib stood out sharply, each labored breath seemed to pull her farther from life.

Eva lay down beside her and sobbed. "Please — a little water — a few drops — please —" *One more hour. God in heaven, give her one more hour.*

T W E N T Y - O N E

FOR THE NEXT week Rachel lay unconscious with a high fever, hovering between life and death. Eva stayed close to Rachel's bed in the new infirmary set up by the Russians, and watched her sister's smallest movement for any sign of change. "God wouldn't have helped us for so long only to abandon us in the end," Rachel had said when Eva was sick; now Eva repeated the words like a prayer, and wept over the psalms in Papa's book. She stayed by Rachel's side until long after the morning visiting hour had ended, when either the doctor or nurse would find her there and order her to leave.

"The camp is not yet free of contagious disease," Dr. Dufkovsky reminded Eva. "It is important that you get as much fresh air as possible, and come here only during the appointed hours."

"Please tell me that she'll live," Eva begged him over and over, but he only replied that it was too early to say, that he wouldn't know until Rachel's fever broke.

"We'll do everything we can, but we have no medicine for typhus," he told Eva. "And her coughing may be serious; I won't know that for a while, either."

When Eva left the quiet infirmary the yard always seemed as noisy as a marketplace. Soldiers ran in and out of buildings with pails of soapy water and cans of powdered insecticide. Jeeps and trucks honked as they drove through the gate with crates of food and supplies. Bonfires burned day and night, fed by blankets and mattresses from the barracks. Women from the town came to distribute clean, used clothing to the girls, who gathered eagerly around the bundles of garments, laughing and teasing one another as they tried on sweaters or jackets.

All day long the Soviet army cooks served hot oatmeal or wheat porridge with sugar, black bread and jam, and strong tea. It seemed to Eva that no matter how often she ate, she was hungry again an hour later.

The girls in the camp were free, but there was nowhere for them to go. They could not leave Trutnov until rail lines and roads were repaired from war damage, the Soviet commander told them, nor could they send or receive mail. Most of the girls spent their days walking in the yard or milling around the tables in the barracks, talking and eating. The kitchen serving area was continuously crowded, as was the shower room, where hot water had been restored. Genia and Tzipora Gelfer led short prayer services every morning and evening. Eva tried to join in, but something in the old prayers always reminded her of home, and often she had to leave in tears halfway through the service.

"What do you think happened to Kayla?" Dora wondered as

she and Eva sat in the yard to drink their tea one day. Dora's infected foot was healing steadily, and she hobbled around on a crude crutch that one of the Russian soldiers had nailed together.

"If anyone can manage, it's Kayla," Eva said, and Dora had to agree.

"If I'd done more for Rosie, or gotten help sooner, maybe she'd have made it," Dora said.

"There was nothing you could do," Eva told her, but the thought only sharpened her fear for Rachel.

"How can I face our family?" Dora asked with tears in her eyes. "How can I tell them: I failed Rosie, but saved myself?" Her family wouldn't blame her, Eva tried to reassure Dora, but she refused to listen. Unable to imagine a future without Rosie, Dora talked endlessly about the past.

"Rosie was the most promising young singer in Lodz," she would say, and she'd recite her cousin's early triumphs once again: Rosie's performance for the mayor; a solo in the school chorus; an invitation from a famous teacher in Kraków who wanted Rosie to be his pupil.

Herr Schmidt rode his bike to the camp daily to study Torah with the rabbi's daughters and to offer help wherever he could. Hundreds of girls signed a petition to protect him, a former Nazi employee, from being punished by the victorious Allies.

"You're free now," Herr Schmidt reminded Eva the first time he came to the camp. "You must learn to think and act like a free person once more." Then he added with a gentle smile, "To begin with, why not leave the camp? To get used to the idea?" When Eva expressed her reluctance to leave Rachel, he promised that he would come to get Eva at once, in the event of an emergency. "It's a small town," he assured her. "You cannot go more than ten minutes away."

So Eva began to take daily walks through Parschnitz, but she did not feel free. Old fears began to surface as Eva traveled streets where she had been forced to march, shouted at by guards, not long ago. What if someone noticed that she wasn't wearing a yellow star? She looked around continuously, half-expecting a German guard to appear. Once she saw a blond woman on a motorcycle, and her heart pounded as she thought for a moment that it might be Frau Hawlik. What's the matter with you? she scolded herself. You're as free as anyone here! But she could not shake the feeling that everyone in town knew she was Jewish and might turn her in to the Nazis at any moment.

On a corner house not far from the camp, a freshly painted sign advertised rooms to rent. Eva often slowed her pace to look up at the clean, white featherbeds hung out to air from a second-story balcony. It might help her to feel like a free person, she thought, if she slept on a real bed and woke up in a bedroom instead of in a barracks. Besides, she reminded herself, the camp was still full of infectious disease. And she would be only minutes from the camp; she could practically see it from here.

One day, after gazing at the featherbeds, she walked up to the door of the rooming house and knocked. The door was opened by a girl about Eva's age, accompanied by a very young boy who clung to her skirts and stared at Eva with wide, black eyes.

"I want a room," Eva said, her heart beating loudly.

"Are you from the camp?" the girl asked cautiously, but without hostility. The boy edged closer to his sister.

"Yes. I can't pay, except —" Eva reached into her pocket for one of the bars of chocolate that the Russian soldiers gave out in endless supply, and which she always carried with her in case she felt hungry. The boy's eyes grew larger when Eva offered him the chocolate, and at a nod from his sister, he grabbed it and began to eat it at once.

"Follow me," said the girl, all reserve gone from her voice. She led Eva upstairs to a bedroom. Through a doorway in the hall Eva caught a glimpse of a bathroom with a deep bathtub on legs, and a flush toilet.

The small bedroom was almost entirely filled by a pine bed. A colorfully embroidered quilt was folded over a small chest, and a narrow door led to the balcony where the white featherbeds hung. Eva ran her fingers over the soft cotton quilt, remembering the quilts she and Papa had carried with them to the ghetto. The room was immaculate, and smelled of pinewood and soap.

"I'll eat my meals at the camp," Eva explained. "In a few weeks — I hope — to be going home. With my sister." She turned her head away to hide her tears.

"You are welcome here as long as you wish," the girl replied. Her brother had already finished the chocolate, and smiled shyly at Eva as she left.

From then on Eva slept on a featherbed in the rooming house, and took long, hot baths in the tub. Her hair was beginning to grow in at the top again, and she took pains to style it so that the thinner part didn't show. She left early each morning to go to the camp, where she ate her meals and waited for the visiting hours at the infirmary.

"Why isn't Rachel's fever going down?" she asked the nurse in tears every day. "She's been like this for over a week."

"It can take a long time. You must be patient," the nurse replied kindly.

"How can she get well if she isn't eating?" Eva demanded, frantic with worry; but the nurse had no answer for that.

Hour after hour through the long May days, Rachel lay unconscious on her bed, with her eyes sunken back in her flushed face. Her stick-thin arms rested on top of the sheet, and her skin was bright red from the typhus rash that had spread everywhere except her face and hands.

"Let me stay a little longer," Eva begged, but the nurse always insisted that she leave at the end of the visiting hour.

"You can't help your sister if you get sick yourself," she reminded Eva. "Go for a walk in the hills. It will do you more good than a dozen walks in town."

So Eva began to walk among the farms and woods just beyond the camp, going a little farther every day. As the days passed, she felt some of her former energy begin to return. At every intersection of the dirt roads, she chose the one that seemed the least used, following it uphill past sheep meadows, hay fields, and groves of trees, until the road narrowed into lit-tle more than a trail.

Among the farms and woods Eva never felt like a prisoner, never worried that someone would identify her as a Jew. She carried bread and chocolate in her pockets, and chose a shady place to stop for lunch before she hiked back to the camp.

By the final week in May, when the Russians had been in the camp for two weeks, Eva was strong enough to walk to the crest of a hill, where boulders and wildflowers filled the meadows. The steep slope and hot sun soon tired her, and at the first thicket of trees she came to, she left the road to sit in their shade. Wild strawberries were ripening at the edge of the woods; after eating her fill of the sun-warmed fruit, Eva tied her kerchief into a pouch and filled it with more strawberries for Rachel.

Then she started off again, following a stream through the woods, past polished boulders and lichen-covered logs and miniature beaches where the sand sparkled as if it were filled with gold dust. Ferns grew in profusion along the bank, and yellow and purple wildflowers sprouted wherever the sun could penetrate the canopy of leaves. The water tasted like melted snow, Eva thought, and she knelt to drink it again and again.

Suddenly the woods ended, opening into a broad, sloping meadow covered with white flowers. Eva waded into the flowers, clustered like bridal bouquets at the top of knee-high stalks. Across the meadow the hill fell away, revealing a lower, rocky knoll, and beyond that, like a rolling ocean, wave after wave of pale green fields interspersed with dark patches of woods. The distant fields were shrouded in haze, making the meadow at her feet seem like something enchanted, from a fairy tale. Eva sat down among the flowers and wept aloud. How could life be so beautiful and cruel, both at once? What kind of world had God created?

Eva had no answers for these questions or for the others that pressed heavily upon her, day and night: who had survived; who would remain of her family?

An image of Rachel as she had looked for the past two weeks — pale, wasted, racked with pain — hovered before Eva. How could she go on without Rachel? In all of Eva's memories, in all her dreams and plans for the future, her sister was beside her. Rachel was as constant, as necessary as the sun and air. Eva lay down in the meadow with her head on her arms, and cried until she fell asleep.

When she awoke the sun was setting, and a chilly breeze swept over her back. What time was it? she worried, shivering as she sat up. She hadn't meant to stay away from the camp this long. What if something had happened to Rachel? Brushing dirt and leaves from her dress, she stood up and started back as quickly as she could.

Long shadows merged on the road as she hurried through the gathering dusk. A church bell rang in the town. Eva began to walk faster. She never should have let herself fall asleep. What if Rachel's fever had gotten worse? What if she died?

By the time she entered the camp gates she was practically running, and almost knocked over a soldier at the entrance to the infirmary. She raced up the stairs to the typhus ward.

Oh, God, no. Dr. Dufkovsky and the nurse were standing at the head of Rachel's bed. Why were they there? What had happened? *Dear God, don't let her die!*

But when Eva reached the bed, Rachel was sitting up, supported by pillows. She was still pale, but her eyes shone with a look that Eva remembered as she slowly smiled and stretched out her arms. Eva threw her arms around her sister and held her close.

"Rachel's fever has broken!" The nurse's words spilled out in a hurried mixture of Czech and German. "Where were you? Herr Schmidt tried to find you hours ago. She's already eaten a bowl of porridge. And two cups of tea!"

"She's past the worst," the doctor told Eva, making notes on Rachel's chart as he spoke. "Her lungs sound clear, too. We will see a rapid improvement now." Dr. Dufkovsky and the nurse left the sisters together, even though the visiting hour was long over.

"God has heard my prayers for you," Eva whispered, leaning her head on the pillow beside Rachel's and keeping her arms around her sister. "We're free now, Rachel," she added softly. "The Germans have been beaten."

Outside the window, the stars were coming out, one by one, like flowers in a dark field. Was Papa looking at them, too? She would not give up, Eva promised herself; not until she knew for certain.

"I brought you something," Eva said, then opened her kerchief and spread the strawberries before Rachel.

They said the prayer together: "Blessed are You, Ruler of the universe, Who brings forth fruit from the earth."

Blessed are You, Who have given me Rachel, Eva added silently.

Some of the old, icy fear started to crack and dissolve in Eva's heart as she watched her sister eating the strawberries. A trace of Rachel's color was beginning to return, and her eyes were no longer sunken or veiled by suffering.

Blessed are You, Who have given us life.

"I feel like a queen," Rachel whispered a minute later, "eating strawberries in bed." She tried to smile, but tears spilled over and ran down her face.

"They're just ripening; soon the woods will be covered with them," Eva said, crying with her. "And I saw meadows full of flowers — whole hills of them, Rachel."

Blessed are You, Who have given us freedom.

"Next time I'll come with you." Rachel closed her eyes and lay still for a long time. Eva waited until she thought that Rachel was asleep, then kissed her and rose quietly to leave.

"Thank you," Rachel whispered, then reached up to wipe the tears from Eva's face.

The long, warm days of May slid into longer, hotter days in June, and Rachel grew a little stronger every day, until finally the doctor said that she was well enough to leave the camp. It was early morning when Eva and Rachel boarded the small passenger train that would take them north toward Poland, toward home. Though the sun had just risen, it had already begun to burn off the mist in the valley, promising a hot day.

Eva's heart started to beat faster as the train pulled away from the Trutnov station. Like the train, her thoughts were bent toward Papa. She was afraid to let herself hope, but she couldn't stop herself anymore than she could stop the engine on the train.

Eva studied her sister's face, no longer hollow-cheeked or pale, and said a silent prayer of thanks that she was not leaving the camp alone. With good food and rest, Dr. Dufkovsky had said, Rachel would be completely better in a few months.

The train clattered over the gray stone bridge and past the mill, now hidden by trees in full leaf. There, two years ago, an old woman had thrown bread and chicken to the Jewish prisoners; there, too, Rachel had given Eva an apple at the end of Yom Kippur. *For a sweet year.* If she closed her eyes, Eva could almost hear the thud of wooden shoes on the stone pavement and the shouts of the guards. It felt strange, like being in a dream, to ride past these places with clean clothes and a full stomach, while the warm sun poured through the window beside her.

Soon the train left the river and headed past the iron gates of the Haase textile factory. The buildings, closed and dark, loomed over the surrounding fields and houses like a sleeping giant that might awaken any moment.

I'm free, Eva reminded herself. *I'm free; I'm alive; I will never go back.* But her pulse raced, and she knew by the way Rachel tightened her grip on her hand that her sister was frightened, too. Eva turned her eyes from the window, and when she looked again, they had already left Trutnov and were speeding through the country, past fields where new crops were growing.

A farmer was pulling a wooden plow by a rope across his chest, turning over the soil between rows of corn plants so small, they looked like grass. A flock of swallows skimmed over the rows just ahead of the farmer, as if showing him the way. Eva watched as long as she could, wondering if this was the field where she had dug a trench for the German army only months ago. But the soil, black and steaming in the morning sun, gave no sign that it had ever been disturbed by war.

"It will still be light out when we arrive in Bedzin," Rachel said.

"We will have plenty of time," Eva agreed, although what they would do in that time, and why a lump formed in her throat just at the thought, she could not have said.

Eva stood up to open the train window, and instantly a fresh breeze blew in, bringing the smell of blossoms and newly turned earth. She was glad that it was summer, when the days stretched out so long they almost merged together. It would be fine with her if there were no night at all, and no sleeping; she had so much she wanted to do, so much she had missed — as if it had been night for two years while she and Rachel were in the camp, and they were just waking up.

They were free and alive and together. The words sang in Eva's head in time to the clatter of the wheels rolling over the track: *free; alive; together.* It was a song of hope, a prayer for everyone she had loved in Bedzin, where they would be by nightfall.

She let out a long breath and settled back for the journey.

E P I L O G U E

EVA AND HER sister returned to Bedzin, where they confirmed what they had feared most: Papa and all of their relatives had been killed in August 1943, when the Germans had rounded up the remaining Jews in the Bedzin ghetto and sent them to Auschwitz.

After a brief stay in Bedzin, the two sisters moved to the Bergen-Belsen refugee camp in Germany, and applied for visas to emigrate to Canada.

During four years in Bergen-Belsen each of them married and gave birth to a son; and each named her newborn Samuel in memory of Papa. In 1949 the sisters and their new families received Canadian visas and emigrated to Alberta, Canada, where they raised their children and built a new life. Eva and her husband, Morris Koplowicz, are living there still.

Eva's son, Samuel, is married to the author of this book.

AFTERWORD:
STORY AND HISTORY

THIS BOOK IS based on the experiences of Eva Buchbinder and her sister in a slave labor camp for Jewish girls and young women in Parschnitz, Czechoslovakia. The sisters were imprisoned there from June 1943 to May 1945.

The camp at Parschnitz, and the factory in Trutnov where the girls worked, were part of a vast system of such camps operated by the Nazi political regime that controlled Germany from 1933 to 1945. Under Nazi rule, Germany conquered most of the nations of Eastern Europe, and proceeded to institute a reign of terror and mass extermination of the Jewish people in each country. The Nazis also imprisoned or murdered members of other ethnic or political groups, including anyone they deemed undesirable to their plan for a "racially pure" Europe. Not all prisoners were sent to labor camps; some camps, such as the large and well-known one at Auschwitz, existed primarily as killing factories in which millions of Jews and other victims were murdered. The period in which the Nazi government carried out its plan of mass extermination is known as the Holo-caust.

In World War II the united military forces of the Allies —including Britain, the United States, and the Soviet Union —fought to free Europe and the world from the oppressive rule of Nazi Germany and their Axis partner nations. The Holocaust ended in the spring of 1945, when the Allied Forces overcame the Axis powers, liberated the surviving Jews and other prison-ers, and restored peace to the world.

The camp in Parschnitz (now called Porici), where Eva and her sister were enslaved, is now a factory of the Kara Fur Com-pany. The factory in Trutnov, where the Jewish girls worked, continues to operate as a textile mill, now owned by A. S. Texlen. Bedzin, a small town in southern Poland, still exists, but Jews no longer live there. A monument marks the place where the synagogue once stood.

ACKNOWLEDGMENTS

THE AUTHOR GRATEFULLY acknowledges the many people and agencies whose kindness and help have made this book possible, and wishes in particular to thank those who follow.

For overall advice, and for careful readings of drafts: Alicia Appleman-Jurman, Gary Young, Donka Farkas, Nina Koocher, Marianne Kent-Stoll, David Frankel, Amy Koplowicz, Mavis Jukes, and Jean and Graham Dragushan.

For expert analysis and direction regarding information contained in the text: Dora Sorell, on epidemic illnesses; Pat Dimmick, of the San Francisco Public Library, on candy-making procedures; Adaire J. Klein, of the Simon Wiesenthal Center Library and Archives in Los Angeles, California, on Jewish religious practice and observance; Elliot Neaman, of the University of San Francisco, on overall historical information and German language usage. The author also acknowledges the help of the Podnikovy Archiv, at the A. S. Texlen factory in Trutnov, Brewster Chamberlin and William W. Hess, of the United States Holocaust Memorial Museum in Washington, D.C., and Sylvie Wittmann, of Wittmann Tours, Prague, for assisting the author in conducting research. Special thanks to Roman Alexander for translating Czech historical accounts of the Nazi era in Parschnitz.

For a grant enabling me to write in uninterrupted solitude: the Dorset Colony House in Dorset, Vermont.

For years of patient help and encouragement: my husband, Sam Koplowicz, and our children, Jordan, Amy, and Sarah.

For invaluable guidance and untiring support: my agent, Gail Hochman, and my editor, Dianne Hess.

Finally, to Eva, for giving me her story, my deepest thanks.

H.F. **DATE DUE**

FOLLETT